Skip Shaughnessy

in

A Score to Settle

Skip's Action Series

Book 5

Marjorie Strebe

Published by:
Marjorie Strebe
Trenton, OH 45067

Interior Design by Marjorie Strebe
Book Cover Design by 100 Covers

Skip Shaughnessy in A Score to Settle / Marjorie Strebe
Library of Congress Control Number: 2026903325
ISBN: 979-8-9902136-5-4
Printed in the United States of America

But I say unto you, Love your enemies, bless them that curse you, do good to them that hate you, and pray for them which despitefully use you, and persecute you.

Matthew 5:44

Table of Contents

Chapter 1

Tossed with the Current

It was a hot day in September, 1995, and off duty patrol officer Skip Shaughnessy was anxious to join his partner at the annual police department picnic. He sprinted back into the house to see what was keeping the rest of his family.

The house was in total chaos.

"Sandy, help Scooter get her shoes on," Erin Shaughnessy, Skip's mom, instructed her third grader.

"Sure Mom." Sandy took her youngest sister by the hand and led her upstairs to find her shoes.

"Suzi, are you dressed yet?" Erin yelled up the stairs to her five-year-old.

"She's coming," called Aunt Rose from upstairs.

Rose's son, Trevor, practically flew down the stairs and raced by Skip on his way out the door. "I got to go. *I'm late for work.*"

"I'm going to the picnic," cried Robby, Rose's younger son. "I want to join that boat race. Skip, is it too late for me to join your team?"

Spinning around, Erin grabbed her son's arm. "Skip, take the cooler of drinks out to the car."

Standing a head taller than his green-eyed mother, streaks of gray highlighting her collar-length brown hair, Skip squinted in the brilliant sunlight that flooded the front room. His dark glasses protected his light-sensitive eyes.

"Relax, Mom. I did it already. In fact, Stephanie, Cassandra, and I have been waiting in the van for nearly five minutes. Are you guys coming?"

"I'm dressed!" Suzi dashed down the stairs and out the door to Erin's mint green minivan. Sandy and Scooter followed her out, scrambling into the back of the vehicle with Suzi.

Aunt Rose trotted down the stairs and joined Erin in the living room.

Erin turned to Rose. "Thanks for helping me to get the girls ready to go. Are you sure you won't join us? There will be plenty of food and fun. And you certainly don't want to stay home by yourself. Even Robby's going."

Rose laughed. "At this point, Robby will follow Skip anywhere." Rose grabbed her purse. "I'll follow you to the picnic. I don't know my way around town yet."

"I'll go with you," said Skip. "That way you won't get lost."

Erin closed the front door of their two-story, red brick home and trailed her son to the van. Skip reached into the back seat and grasped Cassandra's hand. "Come on. We're riding with Aunt Rose."

When they reached the park, Skip watched as the girls scattered, racing off to locate their friends and pair up for the first children's race. Then he and Robby helped the ladies carry the food to the picnic tables. After which, Skip dashed off to locate Officer Jesse Spencer, and Robby raced after him.

Skip and Jesse had been partners for two years, and they were more than good friends. They were like brothers.

"I'm glad you made it," said Jesse. "For a second, I thought I might have to run with Morgan."

Robby cocked his head in bewilderment.

"During the three-legged race," explained Skip. "If you want to race, go find someone that needs a partner."

"Okay," cried Robby in excitement. He promptly paired up with a high school senior who was also looking for a partner.

During the children's three-legged race, the adults paired up for their competition. A brunette woman with a handful of Velcro straps stopped by Skip and Jesse.

"You guys ready?"

Skip smiled. "Yes, miss." The two off-duty patrol officers stood side by side while the girl securely strapped Skip's left leg to Jesse's right.

"Hey, what are you doing?" cried Police Sergeant Brent Morgan. "Spencer, you agreed to run with me."

"Ha-ha, don't make me laugh," said Jesse. "You were only a last minute replacement in case Shaughnessy didn't make it."

"Very funny." Glaring at Skip like it was his fault, Morgan stomped off.

As the adults lined up to race, Skip and Jesse slid their arms behind each other for support. The other officers laughed at them, but when the starting gun sounded, they were the only racers who didn't trip or fall. The boys quickly coordinated their steps and crossed the finish line far ahead of everyone else.

Watching the other teams compete for second place, Skip cheered and yelled for Robby and his pretty little partner, who came in third. But when Morgan tripped and pulled his wife down on top of him for the second time, Skip couldn't help but laugh.

"Be nice, Skip. That could have been me he was knocking down out there," said Jesse.

When the Morgans finally crossed the finish line, Captain Paul Kramer announced the winners through the bullhorn.

"Now our next competition is the boat race," he said. "Remember the rules – four to a boat, no children under 12, and all participants *must wear life preservers.* No exceptions. The course is very simple. Circle around the blue buoy and return to this side of the lake. The first boat team to pass the red buoy finish line marker is the winner. You have fifteen minutes to assemble your teams."

Robby trailed Skip down to the lake. "Skip, can I join your team?"

"Sorry, Robby. We got our team together weeks ago."

"Can I stay and watch?"

"Definitely."

Since Skip and Jesse had already invited Lieutenant Johnny Marshall and Sergeant Kevin McAllister to partner with them in the four-man boat race, their team was complete.

Brent intercepted the veteran officers as they hurried toward their teammates. "You guys can be on my team."

Skip raised an eyebrow at Brent's audacity. Almost everyone intending to race had posted their teams on the bulletin board.

Kevin shook his head. "No way. You couldn't pay me enough to jump into your boat." He darted around Brent and joined his waiting boat partners.

"I'll be on your team," volunteered Robby, dashing over to Brent. "I want to race."

Brent glared at him. "Beat it kid."

Robby turned and walked away, glancing back at Brent one last time before plodding over to Skip.

"Don't let him bother you," Skip said to Robby. "He's rude to *everyone*."

Skip and Robby watched as Brent hurried after Johnny.

"Okay, since Kevin is already committed, it's just you and me guiding my boat. But we can do it. Sheri and BJ will be there to help us paddle."

Johnny slid his hands into his pockets and slowed his pace. "Thanks, Brent, but I can't join your team. Skip asked me two months ago."

Brent slammed his right fist into the palm of his left hand. "I should have known. Skip is like the department pet and needs everyone to look after him. Of course, you and Jesse are his most reliable baby-sitters. Well, I hope he falls out of the boat and drowns." He stomped away.

"Not likely," Johnny called after him. "Skip is a very strong swimmer."

Robby looked at Skip. "Babysitter? What a slam."

With a grin, Johnny joined the others. "He waits until the last minute, then he blames you 'cause I won't join his boat team."

"Yeah, I heard," said Skip.

"But I'd already promised you."

"Besides that, last year his boat tipped over," said Kevin.

Johnny chuckled. "Well, that too."

Robby's eyes widened. "His boat tipped over? It's probably a good thing he rejected my offer."

"I'll say," agreed Skip. "You'd end up in the lake for sure."

As the race preparations got underway for the five competing boats, excited families gathered on the shore to watch the race. Brent's wife and twelve-year-old son climbed into his boat, along with one of the young, female dispatchers. Armed with nothing but oars, ready to launch into the lead, every boat team anticipated the bang of the starting gun.

Cassandra could hardly contain her excitement as she stood on the shore with Robby. They were both there to cheer for Skip.

Skip and Cassandra had only been married for three months. Since Skip's income supported his widowed mother and four younger sisters, Skip was unable to leave home, so when he and Cassandra got married, she joined his family.

Around the same time, Rose Thompson arrived from Los Angeles to visit her brother Stephen, only to learn from Skip that he'd gone home to be with the Lord four years earlier.

Skip introduced her to his mother, and the ladies quickly bonded. Rose stayed with them while Skip worked to reunite her with her two wayward sons.

Robby was easy to work with, but Trevor was headed for big trouble. He stole a motorcycle and got himself into an incredibly dangerous predicament. Then he nearly took Skip down with him. It was nothing short of a miracle that they both made it home safely. Trevor had broken his leg in the ordeal, and he finally got the cast off last week.

Now with Rose and her sons temporarily staying with Skip's family, the house was more chaotic than ever.

Rose had developed a hard, fast friendship with Erin, so she couldn't bear the thought of returning to Los Angeles by herself since both her sons had decided to stay in Forest Valley. Therefore, they were relocating to Forest Valley *permanently*. And Rose had just closed on the house she was buying.

Unfortunately, Rose had responsibilities in LA. As a result, she had spent quite awhile on the phone with the CEO of her multi-million dollar corporation. They discussed the need to relieve her of the many obligations she bore which promoted growth in her business. Then they decided how to divide the tasks among several key chairmen who could best handle them. After that, she could attend quarterly meetings to be kept up-to-date on her business without the headache of running it herself.

Now they were nearly packed and would leave for Los Angeles first thing Monday morning. They'd be gone a week. Rose had already contacted a moving company about packing them up and hauling their furnishings out to their new home in Forest Valley, Wyoming.

Knowing their mother would need their help, Robby took a leave from the Forest Valley college he was attending, and Trevor got permission to take some time off work.

As soon as they arrived in LA, Rose would contact her Realtor about listing her house for sale. She anticipated no trouble selling it.

With the loud crack of the gun, Skip's green boat jumped into first place. It was a close race as the blue, red, and orange boats vied for the lead. But the team members of Brent's yellow boat had difficulty paddling. They worked against each other and coasted in circles. The current created by the other boats rippled against the shore, and the yellow boat drifted toward the middle of the lake.

Meanwhile, the other four boats competed for first place as they cruised around the blue buoy and madly paddled toward shore.

Gathered on the shore, the cheering families screamed and waved their enthusiastic support as the four racing boats drew near. The yellow boat cut circles in the water as it drifted further out into the lake.

That Morgan is something else, thought Johnny. *Everything revolves around him, and he resents Skip for taking the attention he feels rightfully belongs to him.*

Johnny glanced across the lake at the yellow boat, tossed with the current, not going anywhere. He empathized with Brent's hapless crew. Unable to redirect his gaze, he watched, unbelieving, as Brent stood up on the starboard side of the boat. The boat rocked and started to tip. Oblivious to what he was doing, Brent planted his foot on the starboard edge of his boat, and over it went, dumping its occupants into the cold water.

"What a moron," cried Kevin. "That's how he tipped his boat over last year."

He's definitely a slow learner, thought Johnny.

Skip and Johnny immediately slowed their boat and paddled it over to the capsized vessel to pick up Brent's water-logged crew.

"Don't stop now," yelled Jesse. "We're winning. We'll come back for them later."

The green boat rocked gently with the current as Johnny reached over the side and hoisted the dispatcher out of the water. "Some things are more important than winning," he said.

"Thank you, Johnny," she said through chattering teeth.

"Laura, where's your life preserver?"

"Brent insisted we didn't need them. Besides, I can swim."

Skip skimmed the choppy lake for Brent's son, BJ. The boy hadn't surfaced. Stripping off his life jacket, the young officer dived into the lake and swam underneath the capsized boat. Realizing what had happened, the other three boats paddled about to lend assistance. Coming alongside Sheri Morgan, two off-duty patrol officers reached over the side of the red boat and pulled her from the cold water.

"Are you okay, ma'am?"

Shivering, the woman frantically glanced around for her son.

Chapter 2

Stung with Ingratitude

Overcome with a feeling of dread, Jesse watched helplessly as Skip surfaced for a quick breath of air before diving under the yellow boat again. Officer Charlie Curtis shed his life preserver and dived into the cold lake to help Skip locate BJ.

A weak swimmer at best, Brent floundered in the deep water, attempting to reach the side of the blue boat. Gagging on the water he'd ingested, he was about to go under for a third time when Skip grabbed the back of his shirt and hauled him over to it. Leaning over the side, two officers grabbed his arms and lugged him into the boat. Morgan flopped onto the floor like a big fish.

Once again, Skip dived under the water, swimming around the capsized boat while Charlie searched underneath it. As a third officer prepared to jump into the water, all eyes anxiously scanned the rippling lake. Bobbing to the surface with the boy under his left arm, Skip spit out a mouthful of water and drew in a sharp breath.

"I found him." He kicked himself through the water to the orange boat.

Sheri screamed and slapped her hands over her mouth at the sight of her limp son. Charlie's teammate, Greg Foster, lifted the lad into their boat and laid him on the floor, while two other officers pulled Skip into the boat after him. Skip dropped to the floor of the orange boat where Jesse could no longer see him, and the boat took off, slicing through the water at top-notch speed.

The other boats didn't linger. With a hysterical mother aboard one of them, they paddled furiously toward shore. Brent's rescue boat followed at a healthy clip. Skip's teammates picked up Charlie before following them.

Reaching shore, Skip carried BJ to the grassy bank where he continued rescue breathing while awaiting the ambulance. Johnny comforted the boy's mother, who melted into his arms sobbing. Brent looked on helplessly.

Jesse knelt beside the lad and felt for a pulse. "His heartbeat is weak, but it's there."

BJ coughed and drew in a shallow breath.

Ignoring the arrival of the ambulance, Sheri jostled her way through the press, dropped to her knees beside her son, and pulled him into her arms. "BJ, are you all right?"

Captain Paul Kramer parted the crowd. "All right, everyone, let the paramedics through."

The EMS team lifted the youngster onto a gurney and wheeled it to the ambulance. Since BJ was breathing on his own, they permitted his mother to ride with him in the ambulance.

"I'll run home and get us some dry clothes," called Brent. "Then I'll meet you at the hospital."

Brent started toward the parking lot, but Paul detained him. "Morgan, why wasn't that boy wearing a life preserver? Or you? Or Laura? Or your wife?"

"Shaughnessy wasn't wearing one! In fact, neither was Curtis. So why are you singling me out?"

Paul pursed his lips in displeasure. "Shaughnessy and Curtis were wearing them until your boat tipped over. Then they removed their life jackets to swim under *your* capsized boat in search of *your* missing child, because you cannot swim under water with them on. Now why wasn't your team donned in life preservers?"

Brent shuffled his feet and looked away. "I felt they'd slow us down during the race."

"Morgan, you couldn't have gone any slower. You didn't go anywhere as it was. Don't you *ever* let that happen again! You jeopardized the life of every person on that boat, especially your son's. When a person is without oxygen, every second makes a difference, and Shaughnessy had to leave the rescue of your boy to save *you* from drowning. The time he spent rescuing you could have cost BJ his life."

Spinning around, Kramer walked away. He picked up his bullhorn and looked out across the lake where some of his officers had gone to retrieve the capsized boat.

"Hey, Captain, that was an important race," said Charlie, a towel around his neck from drying himself. "How are you going to pick the winner?"

"Good question." Paul gazed out across the lake. "Do you have any suggestions?"

Charlie sighed. "I suppose the only fair thing to do is to give the winning ribbon to the boat in the lead."

Paul laughed. "Fair to who? I don't think anybody will go for that."

Since the winners of the race were entered in a drawing, that left Paul in a quandary. He had no winners to enter. Therefore, he gathered the boat-racing participants to discuss how they should select the winner. There were four boats fighting for first place, and all their occupants were present except Skip, who'd run home to change into dry clothes.

"First off, I want to thank every one of you for choosing to help save some lives rather than win a race. However, now we're faced with a dilemma. How should we choose the winner of today's race?"

"Captain, let's just name the boat team that was in the lead," said Jesse.

"That's not fair!" cried Greg. "Your boat was in the lead, but we were about to pass you."

"I don't think so," said Kevin.

"Wait a minute. Wait a minute," said Tim. "Let's just draw straws."

"That's a game of chance, not skill," said Jerry. "And in no way is drawing straws equal to a boat race."

Paul looked at Johnny, silently pleading for help.

Johnny whistled, bringing instant silence. "You guys are acting like a bunch of ten-year-olds. Look, winning is important to all of us, but don't let it cause you to fight or lose a friend over it. If you haven't figured it out by now, good friends are hard to find. So let's turn this back over to Paul, since we will never agree on what's right or fair, but don't destroy a friendship over it. It's not worth the exchange." With that, Johnny walked away.

After a quick shower, Skip pulled on clean clothes and dry shoes before dashing back out the door and returning to the park. He presumed that he missed the next competition, but he learned that it was scrapped because of the near-drowning incident. Everyone went for the food. After lunch, the children ran to the playground equipment, while some of the adults started a baseball game.

Robby loved baseball, so Skip glanced around for him. Skip knew he'd want to play.

Seeing Brent rejoin the picnic, Skip trotted over to him. "Hey, Brent, how's your son? Is he all right?"

"You've got a lot of nerve. You made me look foolish out there."

"How?"

"By acting like a hero with my boy. I know how to swim. I know CPR. I could have saved him."

"Then why didn't you?" Shaking his head, Skip walked away. He knew that Brent didn't like him, but to distort his intention of rescuing a drowning child left him stung with the man's belligerent ingratitude. Especially when *he* put the child's life in danger by disregarding the rules in the first place.

Hurt by Brent's unfounded allegation, he started toward the ball field and caught sight of Robby, walking hand-in-hand with the young girl who ran with him in the three legged race.

Skip grinned. *Well, he won't be playing ball today. He found himself a girlfriend.*

Captain Kramer hustled up beside him. "You did an outstanding job today, Skip. I just saw you talking to Morgan. He may be crass and a constant irritant to us all, but I assume he thanked you for saving BJ's life."

"Not exactly."

"Well, what exactly did he say?"

"That I made him look foolish for not letting him save his son."

"He couldn't even save himself. I have no idea how he got on with our department, but he's a liability."

"Hey, Skip, are you playing baseball with us?" called Johnny.

"Yeah, I'll be right there." Skip looked back at his captain. "So have you decided how you intend to pick the winners of the boat race?"

"No. Any suggestions?"

"The winning team gets entered in a drawing to win an extravagant home entertainment set. Well, everyone involved in the race forfeited their win when they opted to help save that little boy. Why can't we put everyone's name into the drawing? Let's declare every boat a winner."

Captain Kramer smiled. "I like that idea, Skip. I'll do it."

Skip trotted over to the others who were congregated near the bench to the right of home plate. "Brent, you want to join our team?"

"I would if you weren't on it." Brent hurried to the pitcher's mound and snatched the ball from another officer. "I want to pitch."

Johnny handed Skip the bat. "Do us all a favor, kid. Go put him in his place."

"Well, I..." Skip glanced around at the other officers, all nodding in agreement. "Sure, why not? He can't possibly hate me any more than he already does."

With a smirk, Brent popped out his chest and wound up for the pitch. The bat poised over his shoulder, Skip glanced around the field, deciding where to hit the ball. Brent threw the first three pitches so far above his head or outside the strike zone, he couldn't have reached them if he'd tried.

"Will you swing at something?"

"As soon as you give me something to swing at."

Not wanting to be walked, Skip decided if he could hit the ball, he'd swing. The next pitch was so low, he brought his bat down like a golf club and smacked a line drive right at Brent. The ball shot through his legs and past the second baseman, allowing Skip to easily reach first base.

Skip grinned when Kevin came to bat. If Brent accidentally threw the ball in the strike zone, Kevin would hit it out of the park. Apparently, Johnny lined up all their best hitters for Brent.

Brent glared at Skip and prepared for his next pitch. Skip took a lead, bolting to second the instant the ball left Morgan's hand. The pitch was so wild, the catcher had to chase after it, and Skip advanced to third.

"Shaughnessy, quit stealing my bases," cried Morgan.

While Skip patiently waited for another wild pitch so he could run home, Morgan threw one ball after another, walking Kevin. But Kevin didn't stay on first, either. He took a lead, so Morgan fired the ball to first base. The wild throw sailed over the first baseman's head. When he turned to chase it, Kevin stole second, and Skip stole home.

Brent threw down his glove and stomped off the mound. "That does it. I quit."

Jerking to a stop, he pointed at Skip. "You made a laughing stock of me in front of the entire department. You've had it, Shaughnessy. I'll get even with you if it's the last thing I ever do."

Chapter 3

Vengeance is Mine

With a sigh, Skip looked at Johnny.

"Don't pay any attention to him. He's responsible for his actions, not you. It's always easier to blame someone else than to accept responsibility."

Pouring in from the field, the other team cheered Skip.

Skip smiled at their enthusiastic show of support. Brent was rude to everyone and difficult to work with, so Skip wasn't the only one who tolerated him.

"Well, I'm gonna go find Cassandra. I've hardly seen her all day."

He headed for the picnic tables where Cassandra sat, visiting with some of the ladies. He needed to talk to someone, not that he couldn't talk to Johnny, but the soft feminine understanding she'd offer appealed to him. Straddling the picnic table bench, Skip sat down between Cassandra and Jackie, Jesse's wife.

"I thought you were playing ball," said Cassandra.

"I was." Skip looked across the park where the game was getting underway.

Cassandra grasped his hand and stood. "Come on, Angel. You have something on your mind. Let's go for a walk."

She knew him well. Holding hands, the young married couple hiked down to the path that circled the lake. They quietly strolled around the lake. Scooping up a couple of smooth stones, Skip skipped them across the still water.

"What's on your mind, sweetie?"

He was a cop, and this whole situation was utterly ridiculous. So to unload his unfounded concerns on Cassandra smacked of childishness. He fired another stone into the water, rippling the lake.

"Nothing."

He changed his mind about talking to her. Now he wished he'd stayed to play ball. Even then, he knew his mind wouldn't be on the game.

"Nothing?" Taking his hands in hers, Cassandra faced him. "Skip, you left a baseball game to come find me. You *never* do that. Something's bothering you. What is it?"

"Morgan's constant harassment."

"Who's Morgan? A fellow officer?"

"Yeah. Ordinarily I ignore him, but this afternoon he threatened to get even with me. I don't know if he's blowing off steam or if he plans to set me up."

"Maybe you should tell the captain."

"No way. It's taken a long time for the other officers to accept me as part of the department. If I took this to the captain, they'd all brand me as a tattletale. Since I've joined the department, Morgan's referred to me as a kiddy cop, and he's labeled Johnny and Jesse as my babysitters. I don't need to give him any ammunition."

"Then at least let Johnny know what's going on."

"Johnny knows. He was there."

The final event of the day was the drawing. Although Skip had no use for such an extravagant home entertainment system, his mother could use it. So if his name got drawn, he intended to give it to his mom.

Everyone gathered at the picnic tables, waiting patiently while Police Chief Cory Clark thoroughly shook up a clear plastic, sealed container with all the entries. Removing the lid, he held it out to a young girl and said. "Here, sweetheart, pick one."

With a big grin, the girl reached in and pulled out a name, handing it to him. Silence saturated the picnickers.

Chief Clark cleared his throat. "And the winner of our home entertainment system is..." He paused for effect. "Sheri Morgan."

"Morgan!" groaned a number of people.

"How did her name get into that box?" said Jesse. "She didn't win any event to qualify her to be entered in the drawing."

Skip raised an eyebrow. He didn't know winning that system meant so much to Jesse.

As people scattered, Skip and Robby rounded up the little girls while the ladies packed up the leftover food.

Strolling toward the car, Cassandra snuggled up to Skip. "It was nice that you were off today. I know some officers had to work."

Skip glanced back at the lake. It might take him awhile to shake the fear he experienced at the mere sight of that motionless twelve-year-old, but the boy's dad had him worried. Something told him that Brent would find a way to carry out his threat.

Sirens screamed and spotlights circled the Wyoming State Prison yard. Finally outside the wall, Jason McKenzie ducked into the shadows with the three Brady brothers, huddling near the wall where the lights couldn't reach them. He was glad that they had set up the escape, because he didn't think he'd be able to get away on his own. But he had unfinished business on the outside of those prison walls. He intended to eliminate the boy whose testimony set him up.

Guards ran with their guns drawn as the loudspeaker announced the escape of four inmates. With guards and dogs headed their way, the prisoners bolted through the darkness, trying to avoid the illumination of the spotlights. Gunshots echoed through the uproar.

"Bryan! Roy's been shot," cried Kenny Brady. "We've got to go back for him!"

"No!" shouted the other two convicts.

"We can't just leave him!"

"I'm afraid we have no choice. Right now, we have to think of ourselves. McKenzie, where are you headed?"

"Forest Valley. I have a score to settle."

"Kenny and I will be hiding out with our baby sister. Meet you there, Kenny."

Armed with guns from the guards they'd overpowered, the three men separated to increase their chances of escape.

With a yawn, Skip silenced his alarm before it woke Cassandra. Then he hurriedly got dressed. He'd enjoyed a three day weekend – Friday, Saturday, and Sunday. Because of the stress of his job, he often had three consecutive days off, but rarely did they fall on a weekend.

Cassandra didn't stir as he dropped to his knees beside the bed. Skip always started his day in prayer, especially with his job. But today, his Aunt Rose and two cousins were flying back to California to make arrangements for their final move to Forest Valley. And he wouldn't get to see them before they left. He'd be at work before they got up, and they'd be in California by the time he got home from work.

Skip bowed his head and quietly prayed for their safety and protection as they traveled. Then he prayed for his family, for himself, and for his good friends at work, that God would keep them all safe.

"And, Lord, especially be with Jesse. Open his eyes to see his need for You. Do whatever it takes to bring him to Christ before it is eternally too late. In Jesus' name I pray. Amen."

With tears in his eyes, Skip slowly got to his feet. Then he reached down and gently touched Cassandra's soft cheek before planting a tender kiss on her temple.

"See you after work," he whispered.

Leaving the bedroom, he softly shut the door and started quietly down the stairs, so as not to arouse the whole household.

Skip paused. There was a light on downstairs and soft voices drifted up the stairwell. Either someone was up, or they had an intruder.

Ever so quietly, Skip slipped down the stairs, following the glow of the light and the sound of voices. He stepped into the kitchen.

"Well, good morning, Sleepy Head," said Aunt Rose. "Your mother told us that you leave for work around 5:15, and we wanted to see you before we left."

"Hey, Skip, where's your uniform?" asked Trevor.

"It's in my locker at the police station," said Skip with a grin. "I change at work unless I'm working incredibly long hours, which I was when you guys breezed into town."

"You got time for breakfast?" asked Erin, pouring some batter into the waffle maker.

Skip glanced at his watch. It was 5:08. "I'll make time."

He enjoyed a quick breakfast with his mother, Aunt Rose, and two cousins. Everyone else was still sleeping.

Before he left for work, Aunt Rose kissed him and said, "You take care of your precious family."

Skip cocked his head. "You sound like we'll never see you again."

"Well, we certainly plan to come back, but you know there are no guarantees in life. And we never know when we'll live our last day on earth. Any one of us could go out into eternity before we meet again."

Skip knew that what she said was true, and he pondered her last words to him all the way to work. He pulled into the station parking lot at 5:52.

The moment Skip entered the police station, Jesse hailed him into the captain's office.

"Why's he want to see me?" asked Skip.

"He didn't say, but he wants to talk to you before briefing. He said it's important."

With Morgan's threat fresh on his mind, he stiffened. Something told him that he was in trouble. Forcing a smile, Skip strode to Captain Kramer's office and rapped on the closed door.

"Come in, Shaun."

Skip slipped into the office and closed the door. "You want to see me, sir?"

"Yes. Sit down."

"Am I in trouble?" Skip lowered himself into a chair.

"Not with me." Kramer handed Skip a fax. "However, this came over the wire a little while ago."

With a raised eyebrow, Skip took the paper and started reading. "Attention All Law Enforcement Agencies: Be on the lookout for three escaped convicts; Kenneth and Bryan Brady, and Jason McKenzie."

Skip caught his breath. *Cassandra's dad escaped from prison.* He looked at Kramer without reading the rest of the report. "When did they escape?"

"Last night about 10:00. McKenzie is no doubt on his way to Forest Valley. Not only does his family live here, but so do you. Your testimony convicted him, and he swore to get even. You're in danger if you stay in town."

"I know, but I couldn't live with myself if I ran. And what about my family? Do I leave them here unprotected, or do I take them with me and try to hide them, as well – a family of seven." *At least Aunt Rose, Robby, and Trevor are leaving for Los Angeles this morning,* thought Skip. *And they'll be gone at least a week.*

"Good point."

"But I appreciate the warning, Captain."

"You would have heard it in briefing anyway. I just wanted you to know before I announced it."

"Thank you, sir." Skip pulled open the door and paused. "Captain, this doesn't change anything, does it?

Jesse and I are scheduled to visit my little sister's kindergarten class this morning. We can still go, can't we?"

"I don't see why not. Just stay alert."

Skip detoured to the locker room to change into his uniform. When he entered the briefing room a few minutes later, he found everyone waiting for him.

"Hey, Shaughnessy, you're late," said Brent. "What happened to your babysitters?"

Kramer glared at him. "Shut up, Morgan. Shaughnessy's late because I detained him, and that's none of your business."

With muffled snickers, the other officers glanced at Brent.

Kramer covered the little incidents around town before dropping the big bomb on his officers. "Jason McKenzie was convicted of killing a police officer, so he's extremely dangerous. In addition, he threatened Skip for testifying against him. You guys be on the lookout for these escaped convicts, and remember to provide Skip with all the extra support and protection that you can give him. Be careful out there, Jesse. McKenzie has already killed one cop, so he won't hesitate to kill you to get to your partner."

Dismissed from briefing, the officers filed into the hallway. Skip felt fortunate to be surrounded by such good friends who would keep him covered.

"Now our kiddy cop has a whole department full of babysitters."

Except, maybe, Morgan.

Brent winked at Skip and lowered his voice. "After all, you might need a diaper change when you wet your pants out of fright. But don't worry, Shauney. I'll help them babysit you. Because everyone knows that you're scared to death of McKenzie."

Skip clenched his fists. If Morgan didn't shut his mouth, he'd forget he was a Christian and clobber him right there in the police station.

Just then, Captain Kramer stepped into the briefing room doorway. "Morgan, in my office. Now!"

Skip breathed a sigh of relief when Brent turned toward the captain's office.

"I'm not finished," he called to Skip.

"Yes, you are," said Kramer, following him down the hallway.

As the officers left the station, they congregated under the carport, which housed the blue and white patrol cars.

"Skip, don't let Morgan get to you," said Greg. "Remember, we look out for each other. That's called teamwork."

Kevin nodded in agreement. "And if anything looks the slightest bit suspicious, call for back up. We'll be there in a flash."

"Yeah," said Johnny. "Don't...take...chances."

Climbing into their patrol cars, the officers turned out of the parking lot and headed different directions.

"Skip, how do you put up with Morgan?" asked Jesse.

By the grace of God.

"I'd have killed him a long time ago and pleaded temporary insanity."

I wanted to kill him today. Thank goodness the captain intervened when he did, or I might have slugged him.

"All it would take is one bullet. You could claim that your gun accidentally discharged while it was pointed in his direction."

Skip exploded into laughter.

"Even if the jury found you guilty of negligent homicide, you could get off with a six-month suspended sentence."

"And a police record. No thanks, Jesse. I don't want to mar my Christian testimony on someone who's not worth the bullet. Besides, God says in the book of Romans, 'Vengeance is mine. I will repay.'"

Jesse rolled his eyes. "Well, He sure is taking His time."

With an opening that would lead to his favorite topic, his relationship with Christ, Skip changed the subject, knowing that anything he said would start an argument with his partner. And after dealing with Morgan, he wasn't in the mood to argue with Jesse.

"By the way, Suzi's kindergarten teacher asked me to visit her class this morning. She said that the children have been learning about strangers, and she wants them to know that a police officer is their friend."

"What time?"

"Nine o'clock."

"I'll go with you. With McKenzie on the loose, I think it would be wise if we stayed together."

"I agree. Besides, the thought of being alone right now is a little unnerving. Now, I certainly don't expect anything to happen at the school, but if it does, I want you on the inside with me, helping me to protect those children."

Chapter 4

Skip's Secret

Shortly before nine o'clock, Skip parked the cruiser directly in front of the school building and radioed dispatch of their location. Quietly entering the building, the two officers strolled down the hallway to the open kindergarten classroom door.

"Boys and girls, I have a real treat for you today." Miss Faye, the kindergarten teacher, sat on her desk at the front of the room. "Tell me what very important subject we've been discussing."

Skip and Jesse stepped inside the door. Since no little heads turned around, they knew that the children did not detect their presence.

"That police officers are our friends," said a dark-haired little boy. "But I don't think so. They handcuff you and take you to jail if you're bad. That's what my daddy says. And I'm afraid I'll go to jail, so I run away from the police."

Suzi's eyes widened and she stared in disbelief at her classmate.

Miss Faye giggled at the wide-eyed expression on her face. "Tommy, I think Suzi disagrees with you. You see, there's something very special about Suzi that none of you know. She lives with a police officer."

With startled expressions, the entire class shifted in their seats to look at Suzi.

"Boys and girls, this is such an important lesson that I invited him to our class to talk with you this morning. He's very friendly. He loves children. And he's been looking forward to meeting all of you." Miss Faye motioned for Skip and Jesse to join her at the front of the classroom. "So let's welcome to our class Suzi's brother, Skip."

"Skip!"

Halfway to Miss Faye, Skip caught his little sister when she bounded out of her seat and leaped into his arms.

"Whoa! Suzi, I'm in uniform." He hoisted her above his gun belt. "And I know it's been a long time since I was in kindergarten, but I'm sure the rules haven't changed that much. Aren't you supposed to stay in your seat?"

"Oo, I forgot."

Miss Faye smiled. "Suzi, do you always greet your brother that way?"

"Yes, ma'am. I always do. Skip's the best brother in the whole world."

Skip lowered his young sister to the floor and sent her back to her seat. Leaning against the teacher's desk, he glanced around the room at all the kindergartners. Jesse stood at the back of the room near the door surveying the classroom full of children.

Standing at the front of the classroom, Skip said, "Who can name one of our most important jobs as police officers?"

The boys and girls all looked at one another.

"I can. I can." Suzi waved both hands in the air. "Protecting me. Right, Skip?"

"That's exactly right. And when I'm not available, Suzi knows that she can run to Jesse or any police officer in our department."

"But don't you arrest bad people?" asked Tommy.

"I arrest people who break the law. The laws are there for your protection. If someone breaks those laws, then I arrest them in order to protect you."

"But people that break laws are bad people. My daddy says if I'm bad, I'll go to jail."

Skip raised an eyebrow. "You mean, if you disobey or tell a lie or sneak a cookie before dinner?"

The boy nodded.

"Come here, Tommy," Skip motioned for the youngster to approach him. "I want to tell you a secret. Then we'll share it with the class."

Tommy stiffened and bit his lower lip. Sliding from his seat, the youngster inched his way toward Skip. Skip grasped the child's hand and pulled him close. Then he lowered his voice.

"When I was your age, I did the same things."

"You did?"

"Yes, sir. And I lived with a police officer, too, because my daddy was a cop."

Tommy's eyes widened and his mouth dropped open.

"What's the secret? What's the secret?" chanted the class.

Drawing closer to Skip, Tommy lowered his voice to a whisper. "Did your daddy promise to put you in jail for being bad?"

"No. He never did that to me. When I was bad, he spanked me or sent me to my room, like I've done with Suzi on occasion. But I've never threatened to arrest her for any reason." Skip winked at him. "Now, let's tell the class our secret."

Tommy snuggled up to him. "I don't want to tell them. That's our secret."

"But we promised to share it with them. Remember?" Skip turned the boy around to face the class. Standing with his hands on the lad's shoulders, he said, "Tommy wants you to understand that my uniform doesn't change who I am inside. I'm still Suzi's big brother." He placed his hand over his heart.

As Tommy returned to his seat, all the children started talking at once. Skip clapped his hands, quickly bringing silence. "Now, who wants to be my friend?"

Every hand shot up, including Tommy's.

"And who will let me and Jesse be their friends?"

The children laughed and once again raised their hands.

"Great. Now if it's all right with Miss Faye, you may come outside and see our patrol car."

"Can we go?" begged the children. "Please. Please."

Miss Faye held up her hand, motioning for silence. Once her class had quieted down, she said, "Line up at the door quietly. Other classes are still in session."

The boys and girls hurriedly lined up.

Standing at the door, the teacher put a finger to her lips. "Shh. We must sneak out quietly, so walk softly and no talking until everyone's outside."

The children obeyed, softly following their teacher down the hall and through the main entrance. The first two children in line held the doors open for the rest of the class. Skip and Jesse brought up the rear as they left the building.

"Skip, that was great," said Jesse. "You're really good with kids."

"With four little sisters, I've had loads of practice."

Once outside, the excited youngsters raced down the walk to the police cruiser parked in front of the school building. They gathered around the car peering in the lightly tinted windows.

Reaching the car, Skip opened the back door. "You want to climb in?"

"What's this for?" asked a young boy scrambling onto the hard plastic seat and rapping his knuckles on the Plexiglas that separated the front and back seats. "Why's there a window here?"

"That's for our protection," said Jesse. "That keeps our prisoner from spitting at us or throwing up on us."

Suzi made a face. "Skip, they do that to you?"

"Yeah, sometimes they do some nasty stuff in the back of that car."

Miss Faye looked horrified. "Is it safe for the children to be climbing around back there?"

Jesse nodded. "Yes. We thoroughly scrub down the backseat and disinfect it after incidents and accidents. So it's clean."

"And for most of you who have never ridden in the back seat of a police car, the rear doors don't open from the inside," said Skip.

Opening the driver's door, he slid behind the wheel. The children piled into the car and gathered around him as he showed them the many fascinating features that other cars didn't possess. At their request and with their teacher's consent, he demonstrated the lights and sirens.

"Suzi, did you rode in the police car?" asked Tommy.

Suzi grinned. "Oo, yes. Lots of times. It's fun having a big brother on the police force."

"Can I have a ride?" asked Tommy.

Skip glanced at his watch. "Maybe another time, kid-o. Jesse and I have to get back on patrol. The captain gave us thirty minutes to spend with you kids and we've been here for almost an hour."

Stepping from the car, Skip grasped Tommy's hand. As all the children clustered around him, he took time to shake hands with each of them. "Always remember that we're here to help and protect you. Police officers are your friends unless you are breaking the law. And although it's wrong to disobey your parents or your teacher, we don't arrest children for things like that."

Jesse jumped behind the wheel and Skip slid into the passenger's seat, waving at the children as they coasted down the drive and out into traffic. Barely three blocks from the school, a passing motorist flagged them down. Driving the opposite direction, Jesse pulled alongside the motorist and rolled down his window.

"What's the problem?"

"A few blocks back I passed a crazy man standing in the middle of the street in his shorts waving at cars like a maniac. I think he's trying to get people to pull over."

"Thanks for letting us know. We'll check it out." Jesse accelerated as he continued down the street.

"You think he was pulling our leg?" asked Skip.

"Nope, 'cause there he is."

Chapter 5

Convict on the Loose

Approaching a busy intersection, Jesse pulled over to the shoulder of the road. The man dashed toward the patrol car, shivering and rubbing his arms.

"Help me, please. I've been robbed. I've been *robbed!*"

Skip opened the cruiser's back door, and the man crawled into the warm police unit.

"What's your name?" asked Jesse.

"Fred Brewster."

Resting his left arm on the top of the car, Skip said, "Where are your clothes, Mr. Brewster?"

"They were stolen."

"While you were wearing them?"

"Yes. The guy pointed a gun at me and told me to take off my clothes. What would you have done?"

Jesse handed Fred a blanket he fished from the trunk of the cruiser. "Probably the same thing."

"He said that he needed some different clothes, and mine would fit him perfectly."

Skip caught his breath and looked at Jesse.

One of our escaped convicts, mouthed Jesse.

Skip nodded. *But which one?*

"Then after he stole my clothes, he stole my car."

"Wait a minute," said Skip. "Maybe you'd better start at the beginning."

"I was on my way home from a business trip in Laramie. I live on the other side of town. It was real early, maybe three or four a.m. And out of nowhere, this guy leaped right in front of my car. I slammed on the brakes and nearly mowed him down. I barely got the car stopped when he shoved a gun through my open window and ordered me out of my own car."

"Did you get out?" asked Skip.

"You'd better believe it. That guy had a gun pointed at my head. After I got out of the car, he told me to strip to my underwear. He took my clothes, car keys, and car. He stole practically everything I had – my wallet with over $700 in it, a brief case containing an invaluable address book, and a multi million-dollar contract. He stranded me out in the middle of nowhere bone broke with no way to contact anyone. And it was freezing outside. I walked for hours just to get to town. I needed a phone so I could call the police, but everyone thinks I'm a lunatic running around outside in my shorts."

"What time were you robbed?" asked Skip.

Fred crinkled his nose deep in thought. "Mmm, about 3:40, give or take ten minutes. I was so rattled that I never looked at the clock."

"Where exactly did this happen?"

"Highway 487, approximately fifteen miles south of town."

"Boy, there's nothing out there," said Jesse.

"Can you describe the man?" Skip jotted notes as Fred talked.

"Well, it was dark out and everything happened so fast, but I did get a look at his face. He's Caucasian, brown hair, and brown eyes. And if he changed into my clothes, he's wearing a short-sleeve blue shirt, navy windbreaker, and khaki trousers."

Skip and Jesse exchanged glances. The Brady brothers were blue-eyed.

"And if I ever see that guy again, so help me I'll..."

Jesse interrupted him. "Mr. Brewster, last night three convicted murderers escaped prison. It sounds to me like you were lucky to have escaped with your life."

Skip and Jesse continued questioning Brewster, gathering details on their suspect and the property he'd stolen.

"If this isn't bad enough, I have to tell you that while I was in Laramie, I went hunting with a buddy," said Fred.

"Hunting?" echoed Skip. "So you had firearms in the trunk of your car?"

With a heavy sigh, Fred nodded. "A rifle, a shotgun, and ammunition for both of them."

"Oh, boy," groaned Jesse. "That's a disaster."

A Score to Settle

Skip broadcasted the information over the radio to all units, describing the stolen vehicle, the stolen property, and the suspect.

"Skip, he described McKenzie," whispered Jesse.

"I know."

"Now what?" asked Fred.

"Officer Spencer and I will run you home, Mr. Brewster," said Skip.

"Thank you."

Skip closed the cruiser's rear door and slid into the passenger's seat beside Jesse.

"I sure appreciate this," said Fred. "Only problem is, I'll have no way into the house. I live alone, and my house keys were in my trouser pocket."

"We'll get you in," said Jesse. "What's your address?"

Skip radioed dispatch, requesting they contact a locksmith to meet them at Brewster's house.

By the time the boys returned to the station, it was past lunchtime and Skip's stomach was grumbling so fiercely, he had difficulty focusing on his report. While they were writing, Captain Kramer entered the break room.

"Jesse, you guys verified the ownership of that house, didn't you?"

"Certainly, Captain. We didn't help that guy break into someone else's house. That was definitely his residence."

Kramer sighed. "Morgan's spreading rumors again."

"Does that surprise you, Captain?" asked Skip.

"Nothing he does surprises me anymore." Kramer left.

Word spread that McKenzie was in town, and Skip's apprehension increased. Fearing his young sisters could be a target, he thought it safer to pick them up from school, rather than let them ride the bus.

"Captain, may I run to the school to pick up my sisters? I'll stay an hour later."

"That's all right, Shaun. You're dismissed for the day."

"Thank you, sir."

Skip changed out of his uniform and jumped into his car, racing across town to the elementary school. Seeing his little sisters heading toward their bus, he honked and hollered to them through the open window.

"Stephanie! Sandy!"

Taking Suzi's hands, Stephanie and Sandy ran to their brother's car and scrambled into the back seat.

"Skip, what are you doing here?" asked Stephanie.

"Never mind. I want you girls to play inside today."

"Why?" asked Sandy.

"Girls, do you believe I would ever restrict you for no reason?"

"No," said Stephanie. "We just want to know what it is."

"Trust me, and do as I ask. Okay?"

"We can't even go into the back yard?" asked Suzi.

"No. Do not leave the house."

Big sighs filled the car, followed by a long silence. Finally, Stephanie said, "Okay. We'll play inside today."

The girls clamored through the front door forty-five minutes before their bus was due to arrive, and Skip trailed them into the house an hour before his shift ended.

His sisters scattered. Sandy hurried to the refrigerator. Suzi ran to play with Scooter. And Stephanie traipsed upstairs.

Kicked back in the recliner, Erin looked up from her book when her house became a sudden flurry of activity. Seeing her puzzled look, Skip displayed an impish grin, always known to ward off undesirable questions.

"Did Aunt Rose and the boys get off okay?" asked Skip before his mother thought to grill him with questions about their untimely arrival.

"They did," said Erin. "In fact, they've already landed in LA. Rose called me as soon as they got off the plane."

"That's good to hear." Skip smiled at his mother and trotted up the stairs to his bedroom. He needed time alone to read his Bible and pray. He was still trying to process the unexpected news of McKenzie's prison break.

Slipping into his bedroom, Skip closed the door and grabbed his Bible, sprawling onto his full-sized bed on his stomach to read. He opened to the Psalms, reading several chapters.

He found greater peace in Psalms than in any other book of the Bible. With the Word of God still open in front of him, he bowed his head to talk to Jesus. Skip desperately needed wisdom. How could he tell his wife and mother the news? He knew that the knowledge of McKenzie's prison break would increase the worry that his anxious mother already experienced due to his job, but he had no clue how Cassandra would respond.

"Skip?" Cassandra pushed open the closed bedroom door and stepped into the room, closing the door behind her. She crossed the room to the bed and sat down beside him, gently rubbing his back. "You want to talk about it, sweetie?"

"Talk about what?" Skip looked up at her.

"Whatever has caused you to isolate yourself from the rest of us. Your mom said that you picked up the girls from school and walked in the door ninety minutes early this afternoon. Did something happen at work?"

Skip shook his head. "No. I just needed some time alone with the Lord."

"All right, Angel. Well, I'll leave you alone, then." Cassandra patted his back and left the room.

Staring after her, Skip wondered if he should tell them before they learned about it from the media. *Maybe they'll catch him tonight. Then I won't have to tell them at all.*

Brent Morgan escorted his wife and son into a restaurant. As they prepared to order, he caught sight of Jason McKenzie standing at a table across the room, talking to a young couple with a baby.

Shoving the menu into his wife's hand, Brent leaped up. "Order for me."

Without waiting for a reply, he dashed into the restroom. Hopefully, McKenzie didn't see him, cause if he did...

The bathroom door squeaked open. Without waiting to see who entered, Brent ducked into a nearby stall and bolted the swinging door. The restroom patron turned on the water, allowing it to run for a moment. Then he turned it off and hit the dryer button.

Brent heaved a sigh of relief. *It just sounds like some guy washing his hands.*

With the dryer still running, the restroom door squeaked open and quietly closed again.

Good. Whoever was in here left the restroom. Brent slowly opened the stall door and stepped out of the stall. McKenzie seized him by the shirt collar and slammed him against the wall.

"I ought to smash in your face for double-crossing me." Clenching Brent's shirt collar, McKenzie slammed his head against the bathroom wall, giving him an instant headache.

"Why would I double-cross you?" With McKenzie choking off his windpipe, Brent's voice squeaked.

"Don't be a smart-alec. You supplied me with drugs. Have you told your wife how you could afford all the wonderful things you bought for her? Did you tell her that you purchased her precious things with drug money?"

Gazing into McKenzie's bloodshot eyes, Morgan swallowed hard. He suspected that his whole life was about to unravel.

McKenzie lowered his voice. "And after being my supplier, you had the audacity to get on the witness stand *in uniform* and lie about me!"

I'm dead now. His life was unraveling at this very moment. In fact, it started falling apart at the picnic. *All because of Shaughnessy.*

"Maybe so, but it wasn't my testimony that convicted you. It was Shaughnessy's kid. He's the one you need to go after."

"I'm having trouble locating him, so you may have to do."

Brent gagged when McKenzie tightened the grip on his shirt collar. "He...he works at the police station."

McKenzie smashed his head into the wall again.

"Stop, and I'll tell you where he lives."

"Where?"

"On the other side of town in that upperclass subdivision near the mall. That's all I know."

Shoving Brent aside, McKenzie left the restroom. Brent stumbled into the wall, banging his head again.

"Ouch."

Allowing himself a moment for his headache to subside, he studied his reflection in the mirror, looking for marks or bruises on his face. Sheri must never know what he'd done. Satisfied that he looked okay after his encounter with McKenzie, Brent returned to his family.

"What was that about?" asked Sheri. "Who was the man that followed you into the restroom?"

"Last night, three convicted murderers escaped prison, and one of them is here in town, trying to locate Shaughnessy."

"Is that the officer who saved BJ's life yesterday?"

"The kid who made a fool of me at the picnic? Yeah, that's him."

"Made a fool of you? Brent, what are you talking about? He rescued our son."

"I could have saved him, Sheri. I'm tired of looking like a fool in front of the entire department. Shaughnessy's in for some real trouble, and this time I'll be the hero. When I save his hide from being burned by that escaped convict, Captain Kramer and Chief Clark will respect me. He's their pet, and I can't stand him. I just want to see the look on his face when I save him for a change."

With a heavy sigh, Sheri glanced from her son to her husband. "Brent, that kind of talk will get you killed."

"I'm a cop, Sheri. I can take care of myself."

"And what about Officer Shaughnessy? He's much younger and far less experienced than you."

Brent grinned. *That's what I'm counting on.*

Chapter 6

A Close Call

Skip found it difficult to sleep with an escaped convict searching town for him and Morgan's threat fresh on his mind.

Cassandra snuggled up to him and rested her head on his chest. "What's wrong, Angel?"

Skip wrapped his arms around her, not certain how to tell her about her dad's prison break or even if he should.

"Come here, sweetie." Rolling to her back, Cassandra pulled him into her arms.

As much as Skip feared his father-in-law, he felt certain that McKenzie would never harm his daughter. Secure in her arms, he finally drifted to sleep.

A Score to Settle

Sitting in a stolen black Oldsmobile, Jason McKenzie staked out the police station from a side street waiting for Shaughnessy to arrive for work. He'd been sitting there for over an hour and the dawn had finally broken the darkness.

It had been four years since he'd seen the sixteen-year-old boy whose testimony convicted him. Hopefully, he recognized the lad. He didn't know what kind of vehicle Shaughnessy drove, nor what shift he worked. For all he knew, the boy did third-shift janitorial work for the department. Then again, maybe he worked second shift in dispatch. Jason never thought to ask Brent what kind of job he held at the police department. Not that it mattered. He'd wait all day if he had to.

Pulling out a pair of binoculars he'd found in the trunk of Brewster's car, Jason peered through them, following cars that turned into the police station parking lot. He grinned, studying the blond driver in the Buick that turned into the lot. Although he wore sunglasses, Jason still recognized him.

Since Jason had been convicted, this was the first time he got to see the boy that testified against him. He was a good-looking boy, taller and more filled out.

Jason lowered his binoculars. "He's just a kid. I should go after Morgan."

But Morgan's words reverberated in his ears. *It wasn't my testimony that convicted you. It was Shaughnessy's kid. He's the one you need to go after.*

And at this point, Jason agreed. But when should he go after the lad? He was now at work. The boy drove around to the rear of the building where Jason could no longer see him. He would soon enter the safest building in the entire city.

Jason frowned and lowered the binoculars. "That's just great."

But he'd waited this long. He wasn't going to give up now. So he continued to study the front of the building through the binoculars.

Jason studied the exterior of the police department, considering where he should plant himself to stake out the parking lot. When the kid left the station at the end of the day, he could pop him with a single shot to the heart. After all, he'd found Brewster's firearms and ammo in the trunk of his car. And he still had the gun that he'd taken from the prison guard.

Drumming his fingers on the steering wheel, he glanced at surrounding structures to see where he could sit and watch and wait. He didn't find a spot that he felt would make a good sniper position.

Releasing a sigh, he brought his hand to his chin. As he pondered his next move, several police cars turned out of the lot. Jason peered through his binoculars and gasped when he saw Shaughnessy sitting in the front passenger seat of a police cruiser.

He's a cop. Somehow, that thought had never occurred to him. A single shot won't do. The shotgun might work better. Cranking the engine, he started the car and pulled out into traffic, maneuvering his vehicle behind the cop car carrying his target.

Catching sight of the black Oldsmobile that trailed them, Skip thought of Fred Brewster. He had a black Oldsmobile. Watching the car through the cruiser's side mirror, he struggled to read the license plate. The vehicle was too far back.

"What's the matter?" asked Jesse.

"I think that black Olds is following us."

Jesse glanced in his rear view mirror. "Mr. Brewster had a black Oldsmobile. I'll swing around. See if you can catch the license number."

When traffic cleared, Jesse spun the car around and passed the Oldsmobile heading the other direction.

"Got it." Skip jotted down the plate number before snatching up the mic and radioing dispatch with the license check.

Jesse circled the car around again, intending to pull up behind the vehicle in question, but it had disappeared. "Wonderful."

Dispatch responded with the information that Skip requested. The car was registered to Fred Brewster and had been reported stolen.

Suspecting McKenzie as the driver, Skip radioed for assistance while Jesse cruised in and out of side streets looking for the stolen vehicle. The longer it took them to locate that car, the more unnerved Skip felt. He and Jesse continually scanned the streets. The cruiser coasted around the corner into an alley.

"Duck!" cried Jesse.

Skip dived under the dash, radioing dispatch that they were under fire just as an exploded shotgun shell sprayed their car. Shattering glass from Jesse's side window showered them, while the cruiser lurched forward and plowed into the side of a brick building.

Grasping the steering wheel shifter lever, Skip threw the car into park before pushing open his car door. He yanked out his gun and dropped to the street in a squatting position, taking cover behind the car. But the high-pitched squeal of tires and the roar of a car engine echoed through the alley. The suspect vehicle raced off before Skip caught a glimpse of it.

Oh, my gosh, was that ever close. Thank you for protecting me, Lord. "Jesse, are you okay?"

Lying over the console between the seats, Jesse slowly sat up and brushed the shattered glass fragments off his uniform onto the floor of the car. "Are we still alive?"

The windshield had multiple cracks.

"Yeah. Thanks for the warning."

Skip heard sirens in the distance and knew that every police car in town was probably racing to get there. Rising to his feet, he keyed his mic, reporting the shooting suspect's last known location and a possible description of the vehicle before he requested a tow truck for their damaged cruiser.

Less than a minute later, police cars streamed into the alley from both directions and officers leaped from their cars, dashing to Skip and Jesse.

"Hey, you guys okay?" asked Tim.

Skip nodded. "Yeah, which is more than I can say for our car. I take it, no one caught the guy driving the black Oldsmobile."

"No," said Kevin. "We saw no sign of any car matching that description when we arrived. Which way did it go?"

"I don't know. It got away too fast." Skip looked at Jesse.

"Don't look at me. It's not my fault. We were lucky that we weren't killed."

It wasn't luck that kept us safe. It was You, Lord. Help Jesse to see that, and show him his need for a Savior.

Jesse's eyes narrowed. His steady gaze made Skip feel like his partner could read his thoughts. "Don't say it. Don't even *think* it."

"Say what?" asked Kevin, glancing from Jesse to Skip and back to Jesse. "What isn't he supposed to say or think?"

Skip knew. Jesse didn't want him to credit God with saving their lives, even silently.

While waiting for the department tow truck, Kevin pulled Skip aside, questioning him thoroughly and gleaning as much information as he could recall from the moment he spotted the Oldsmobile until backup arrived in the alley. Tim talked to Jesse.

"Skip, the car was blasted with a shotgun," said Kevin. "How did the front end get smashed in?"

"When McKenzie opened fire ..."

"Do you know for a fact that it was McKenzie? Did you see the driver? Did you even see the shotgun blast come from the black Oldsmobile?"

"Uh ... no." Skip drew in a sharp breath and started over. "When the shooter opened fire, we ducked so fast that Jesse didn't have time to break or shift to park. In fact, the car jerked forward, so he must have accidentally leaned on the accelerator."

When the police department tow truck finally arrived, the officers were just finishing their on-scene investigation and the cruiser was hooked up. Skip and Jesse jumped into the cab of the tow truck, and the driver gave them a lift back to the station before towing their car into the garage.

It was easy to escape police detection. Leaving the alley before that fleet of police cars arrived, Jason crossed the street and pulled into a nearby supermarket parking lot full of cars. He squeezed between a black pickup truck and a black van, positioning his vehicle so he could watch the activity in the alley across the street.

Within minutes, blue and red flashing lights lit up the street as a half dozen police cars screeched to a stop in the alley.

Jason waited anxiously for the arrival of a rescue squad, knowing he had to hit at least one of those cops. But after awhile, the damaged cruiser was towed off, and the police left the scene.

A Score to Settle

Jason pounded the steering wheel with his fist. Apparently, neither of those cops were injured, and they got by him because he was watching for an ambulance or rescue squad. Well, he knew where to find them. They returned to the police station. But how long would they be there? Twenty minutes or the rest of their shift?

Cranking up his car, Jason left the parking lot, returning to his surveillance position at the police department. That boy would eventually leave the building, and when he did, Jason would be ready for him.

Jason trotted around to the back of the car and deposited the shotgun and shells into the trunk.

"This will work better." Grabbing out the rifle, he slammed the trunk and hopped back into the car. "He won't escape this time. Nor will they see me. I'll do a better job of tailing them."

Chapter 7

Who's to Blame?

Collecting their paperwork, Skip and Jesse sat down in the break room to write their reports.

A few minutes later, Kevin entered the room. "You guys okay?"

Jesse glared at him. "No. *You* let McKenzie get away."

Skip looked up in surprise.

"Wait a minute," said Kevin. "You were right there on the scene and *I* let him get away? And are you sure it was McKenzie? Did you actually see the vehicle *and the driver?*"

"I didn't have to see him to know who it was."

"Jesse, I'm just as certain as you and Skip that the driver was McKenzie, but when we finally catch him we need *proof* to take to court."

"An escaped convict makes Swiss cheese out of our car trying to kill us, and you stand there making excuses. You're the officer in charge, and *you let him get away.*"

Kevin stormed out of the break room and slammed the door.

Skip jumped and looked at his partner. "That was uncalled for, Jesse."

"Says who, church boy? You claim to trust in God. Where was He when we were almost killed an hour ago?" Snatching up his report, Jesse left the room and slammed the door behind him.

Skip stared after him. He had never verbally shared his faith in any way with his partner, so Jesse's outburst stunned him, and he felt it was unwarranted. But although he'd never talked to Jesse about God, he knew that his life was a living testimony that his partner couldn't escape.

Bowing his head, Skip prayed softly. "Lord, I'm scared. Surround Jesse and me with your angels. Protect us in every situation, especially now with danger so imminent, and help us catch McKenzie before he kills someone. In Jesus' name, amen."

The door opened, and the captain strolled in. "Skip, are you all right?"

"Yes, sir, I'm fine."

"Good. Jesse told me that he just unloaded on you and Kevin."

"He did. Captain, may I have my own car?"

Kramer raised an eyebrow. "I don't think so. With McKenzie still at large, I'd rather keep you partnered with someone."

"I'm concerned that anyone with me is endangered. And I don't want to see Jesse get hurt because of me, or anyone else for that matter."

"I understand that. When you're finished with your report, stop by my office, and we'll talk about it."

Certain the captain would agree with him, Skip completed his report and hurried to his captain's office, but he found the door closed. It sounded like a conference in session. Skip knocked softly.

"Come in, Skip. We've been waiting for you."

Skip pushed open the door and his eyes widened at the sight of first shift crammed into Kramer's office.

"What's going on?" asked Skip.

"Call it a delayed briefing. Come in, and shut the door."

Skip slipped inside and closed the office door behind him.

"We have a problem," said Captain Kramer. "His name is Jason McKenzie. He's an escaped convict at large, last seen right here in Forest Valley, and he's after one of our officers. I thought I covered this yesterday morning but I guess I'm mistaken, so we'll go over it again. When we leave this building and go on patrol, who's on his own out there?"

"No one," said Officer Sally Sebastian.

"That's right, Sally. No one. Now, no one wants to die out there, but when a fellow officer is in trouble, everyone rushes to his..." Kramer winked at Sally. "...or her aid. Isn't that right, Skip?"

"Oh, yes, sir."

Kramer's gaze locked with Skip's. "I can't let you have your own cruiser to protect my other officers should McKenzie corner you again. Yesterday morning, I instructed everyone to give you all the support and protection they possibly could. We can't do that if you're allowed to throw out your most valuable asset, which is your partner."

Skip looked over at Jesse. Leaning against the captain's desk, hands in his pockets, he stared down at the floor.

"But Jesse considers me a liability right now, Captain, and he'd rather not be my partner."

"That's not true." Jesse looked up at Skip. "The captain's right, Skip. Had you been alone when McKenzie riddled the cruiser with a shotgun, you likely would have been killed. I saw it coming before you did, and I warned you."

"Skip, I hope you see where we're coming from," said Captain Kramer. "If I give you your own cruiser and you're killed or injured in a conflict with McKenzie, we will always wonder if the presence of another officer would have prevented a needless tragedy. Now, everyone is with you. This meeting is adjourned. Get back to work, all of you."

Skip was never so disappointed in the outcome of a meeting, and he was hurt by Jesse's comments. He thought they were good friends. But good friends don't slam something precious to you, like your faith, even when they don't agree with you. Jesse called him *church boy*.

Trailing Jesse out to a new patrol car, Skip silently slid onto the front passenger's seat and rested his elbow on the window ledge. He gazed absently out the side window. Jesse cranked the car engine and pulled out into traffic. After several long, silent minutes elapsed between them, Jesse finally spoke.

"Are you mad at me?"

"Why would I be mad at you?" Continuing to gaze out the side window, Skip spoke softly.

"Come on, Skip, I know what you're thinking. You're mad at me for blaming God."

"Oh? Were you blaming God? Here I thought you were mocking my faith. What was I thinking?"

Jesse heaved a sigh. "Look, Skip, I'm sorry about the things I said to you and Kevin. You're right. They were definitely uncalled for. I'm just scared. McKenzie's still on the loose."

"Don't you think I know that?" Skip looked at Jesse. "It bothers me that I may not be his only target. I have four little sisters, ya know."

"He won't go after them."

"How do we know that? He wants me. Did it ever occur to you that he might grab one of them to get to me?"

Jesse drew in a sharp breath and glanced over at his partner. "No, it didn't. Forgive my insensitivity. You're my best friend, Skip. I would give my life to protect you.

Now, we're in this thing together, no matter what happens or how this turns out."

"You mean that?"

Jesse held up his right hand and Skip clasped it. "Yes. Like brothers."

Skip glanced around uneasily. "Jesse, this may sound ludicrous, or possibly even paranoid, but I have a strange feeling we're being followed again."

Jesse glanced around. "I don't recognize any vehicles around us. Are you sure?"

"No. It's just a feeling."

Sitting in his car for over an hour, Jason watched the police station through his binoculars, waiting for Shaughnessy to leave the building. Finally, the young officer walked out with his partner.

Jason followed him with the binoculars. "Amazing. I blasted his car with a shotgun and that boy escaped without a scratch."

Setting aside the binoculars, Jason put his car into gear and maneuvered onto the roadway. This time, he followed the police car discreetly, from a distance, blending in with traffic.

For nearly an hour, he played hide and seek behind car after car while looking for an opportunity to plug that cop with a bullet.

Now, how am I gonna corner him out here? he thought. *To shoot him on a crowded city street would be suicide. The cops would kill me in a heartbeat.*

With that in mind, Jason decided to discontinue tailing the patrol car before the cops spotted him again. Flipping on his right turn signal, he changed lanes and coasted around the corner onto Marble Street. Immediately, he turned left onto Courtney Place and pulled over to the curb. He needed a moment to consider his next course of action. He had to think this through.

Skip jumped when his silent radio crackled to life. "Any available unit in the vicinity of Race and Marble, identify."

"Grab it, Skip. We're only a block away."

Skip keyed his mike. "Unit ten's available. We'll handle the call."

"Respond to 1311 Courtney Place to assist an expectant mother while the ambulance is en route."

"Copy." Skip jotted down the address.

Jason had barely stopped his vehicle when, straight ahead, he spotted a police cruiser heading toward him.

"No." Snatching up his binoculars, he peered through to get a good look at the officers in the car. "This is too good to be true."

A Score to Settle

Tossing aside his binoculars, he snatched up his rifle and rolled down his side window. The squad car braked to a sudden stop at the opposite curb in front of a ranch-style, brick home.

Jason took careful aim. He planned to hit his target with a single shot, and he did not intend to shoot the wrong cop.

As the officers approached the front door, the door swung open and a man ran out, giving him one more unintended target.

Although Jason considered himself a fairly decent shot, he also knew it had been a good five years since he'd picked up a rifle. In addition, he had to aim and shoot quickly, before Shaughnessy reached the house. And if either of those two men stepped between his rifle and his target, or Shaughnessy entered the house before Jason got off his shot, the opportunity would be lost. He had *one shot*. He had to make it count.

Holding his breath, Jason steadied his rifle and pulled the trigger.

Chapter 8

In Need of an Ambulance

Halfway up the walkway, the front door burst open and an agitated man dashed out to meet them.

"Thank goodness you got here quickly."

The crack of a gunshot exploded through the air.

"In the house!" cried Skip. "Move it!"

He and Jesse bolted toward the door. They grabbed the stunned father by the arms and hustled him into the house ahead of them. Skip shoved the door closed and threw the deadbolt.

"Lock the back door," ordered Jesse. "Close the windows, and pull all the shades and curtains."

As the home-owner leaped to action, Jesse radioed dispatch, informing them that shots had been fired, and the location of the assailant was unknown. He requested back-up and advised that approaching officers needed to exercise extreme caution.

Lowering his rifle, Jason heaved a frustrated sigh. He missed. Of course, he missed. From half a block away, he aimed at a moving target, rushing to get off a shot while his target was still visible.

In the distance, he heard sirens. Jason set down the rifle and cranked the car engine. Undoubtedly, back-up police units were en route, and he had no intention of lingering. He completed a u-turn and headed back the way he'd come. Turning onto Marble, he passed a rescue squad flying past him with lights and sirens.

An ambulance got called? I wonder if I hit that other man. I know I didn't hit either of those two cops.

Jason pursed his lips in thought. "This is a waste of time. To try and corner him while he's at work is futile. He wears a vest. He carries a gun. He has a police radio on his belt and immediate back-up is available to him. I need to trap him when he's off-duty and alone."

With the house secured, Skip peeked through the curtains. The ambulance sat at the curb directly in front of the house, but the paramedics had to wait for the police to secure the scene. Unfortunately, Skip and Jesse were not in a position to help secure the scene.

The wail of a young woman drifted from the bedroom.

"What are we going to do? We have to get my wife to the hospital. She could deliver any time."

Jesse shifted the curtain and took a quick look outside. "Believe me, there's nothing I'd like better than to turn this over to the medics, but there's a sniper out there. The ambulance is here, but the paramedics are holdup in their truck for protection."

The woman screamed again. "Dirk, help me. Oh, Dirk, the baby's coming!"

"Oh, my gosh. What do I do?" Dirk ran to the front door. "Somebody, tell me what to do?" He dashed toward the kitchen.

"Dirk."

"Do either of you guys know how to deliver a baby?" Dirk turned in circles.

"Dirk!"

Skip glanced from his weak-kneed partner, on the verge of hyperventilating, to the panicked father, who was about to pass out. Although his academy training included a class in basic first aid and childbirth, he didn't cherish the thought of having to put into practice what he'd learned. But the academy instructors included that class for this type of circumstance, and someone had to take charge of the situation.

Skip draped his arm around Dirk's shoulders and guided him into the bedroom, closing the door behind them. "Calm down, and we'll get through this together. Now what's your name?"

"Dirk Benson. I...I...I don't know the first thing about delivering a baby."

"You just do what I tell you. Bring me a sheet or blanket. Quickly."

Dirk rushed a sheet to Skip and helped him prepare his wife for delivery.

Skip smiled at Dirk's wife, calmly removing his wedding band and wristwatch before rolling up his sleeves. "My name's Skip. What's your name?"

"Carrie."

"Well, Carrie, the paramedics will get here as quickly as possible." Skip grabbed a pair of thin rubber gloves from a small pouch on his gun belt and pulled them on.

Breathing through another contraction, Carrie gasped, "Well, I can't wait any longer."

That told Skip that on the next contraction, she intended to push. That gave him approximately thirty seconds to prepare himself mentally and emotionally for this event. And his heart raced, recalling the details of that class, and knowing full well what he needed to do.

Carrie groaned with another contraction. Reaching for Dirk, she clasped his hand and her face turned red as she pushed.

Jesse paced the floor, empathizing with Skip's predicament every time he heard that woman scream. How could he have done that to his partner? As the senior officer, he should have taken charge, not dumped it on Skip. Peeking through the curtains again, he keyed his mic and radioed the back-up units to find out what was happening outside.

"Did you locate the sniper?"

"No," responded Kevin. "We've covered that house from every angle. He must have taken off before we arrived, or we would have seen him."

"Well, we have a woman in labor in here. Is it safe to send in the paramedics?"

"Yeah, I think so."

Jesse's head snapped toward the bedroom when he heard a baby cry. Bounding to the front door, he unbolted it and swung it wide open for the paramedics before hustling to the closed bedroom door. With a soft knock, he pushed open the door a crack. "Is it safe to come in?"

"Yeah, it's safe."

Jesse entered the bedroom, followed by two medics wheeling a gurney that carried a case of medical equipment and supplies. They hurried to Skip, who cradled the tiny newborn in a pink baby blanket. Opening the blanket, the medics tied off the umbilical cord and cut it.

Skip expected them to take the baby from him, but they didn't. They allowed him the privilege of presenting the newborn baby to her mother. Wrapping the baby tightly in the blanket, he laid her in Carrie's arms.

"Thank you, Skip. We shall call her Skipper, in honor of the officer who delivered her."

"How many babies have you delivered?" asked Dirk.

With a grin, Skip held up his right index finger. "One, and you're holding her." Peeling off his gloves, he stepped into the bathroom to wash up.

Now that the heart-pumping, adrenaline-rush of the situation was over, Skip sobered as he considered how close that bullet came to hitting someone. It ripped between the three of them. The bullet meant for him could have killed Dirk or Jesse.

Returning to the police station shaken, Skip hardly said a word to his partner. How could he live with himself if someone else got hurt because of him?

"Hey, are you all right?" Jesse spun the car into a nearby parking spot and they entered the station through the back door. "Skip?"

Skip nodded, then he shook his head. "I don't know." Entering the break room, he snatched up the paperwork he needed and sat down to write his report on the incident. Unfortunately, he found it difficult to focus. He stared at the blank paper, tapping his pen on the table. His mind wandered from McKenzie's threat to his unprotected family to his unsaved partner who nearly got shot today.

A moment later, Captain Kramer and Johnny strolled into the break room. Skip looked up at them.

Paul pulled out a chair near Skip and sat down. "Jesse told me what happened outside the Bensons' home. Maybe I'd better reassign you to the desk until McKenzie's back in custody."

With a heavy sigh, Skip nodded. "Yes, sir. Anyone near me is endangered."

"Right now, I'm concerned about your safety. Why don't you write your report, and then we'll talk about it." Kramer left the room.

Skip looked at Johnny. "What are you doing here? I thought you were off today."

"I stopped by the station for something and ran into Jesse out in the hall. He told me what happened." Johnny pulled up a chair and crossed his legs comfortably.

"I'm scared, Johnny. This guy is relentless. I fear he may go after my family to get to me. How can I safeguard my mother and little sisters?"

"You can't."

Skip raised an eyebrow.

"God will protect them. In the book of Psalms, David said, *'The Lord is my light and my salvation: whom shall I fear?'* In Psalm twenty-three, he says, *'Yea, though I walk through the valley of the shadow of death, I will fear no evil: for thou art with me.'* As long as you're walking close to God, He promises to be with you through the most difficult and challenging circumstances. What does Psalms 4:8 say?"

"'I will both lay me down in peace and sleep, for thou Lord only makest me dwell in safety.'"

"Who keeps you safe?"

"The Lord."

"And Who will keep your family safe?"

"The Lord."

"That's right. Now let's pray and ask God for his peace and comfort in this situation."

Skip smiled. "Thanks, Johnny. I'd like that."

Leaning forward in his chair, Johnny rested his arms on his knees and bowed his head. "Dear Lord Jesus, you know better than anyone what Skip is going through. Give him Your peace and power, discernment, direction, and wisdom to make the right decisions, not just for himself, Lord, but for all involved. For his family, his partner, and the citizens of this town whom he serves so unselfishly. Send a host of angels to surround and protect him and his family. And help us to recapture McKenzie and the Brady brothers before anyone gets hurt. These things I pray in Jesus' name. Amen."

"Thanks, Johnny. Incidentally, if you run into Cassandra or my mom don't mention this incident. They don't know about McKenzie's prison break."

Johnny's eyes widened. "You're kidding. Surely they've seen the news or caught the headlines by now."

Skip furrowed a brow as the headline news raced through his mind. "You're probably right, but neither of them has mentioned it."

"I'm sure they figured you knew, and I doubt that either of them are considering the danger you're in with him loose." Johnny stood. "Well, I got to run. Seriously pray about God's direction. He might want you back out on the street with Jesse. Jesse doesn't realize it, but God is working on his heart. And believe me, God can protect you from anything or anyone."

"I know He can, Johnny. I appreciate you keeping me mindful of something I never should have forgotten from the start. Thanks for your encouragement and prayers."

"Anytime, kid-o." Johnny left.

Skip bowed his head and prayed. "Dear Jesus, thank you for sending Johnny at such a crucial time. Give me direction and fill me with your peace. And, Lord, please take care of Morgan for me. He intends to set me up, if he hasn't all ready."

Chapter 9

Wrapped in God's Peace

Wrapped in the warmth of God's peace, Skip started on his report. When he finished, he headed to the captain's office and tossed his report into the box on Kramer's desk.

Paul leaned back in his chair and looked up at Skip. "Have you decided what to do?"

"The decision's mine?"

Kramer nodded. "I would prefer to temporarily assign you to the station for your protection, but I know that you have faith in God and might feel like I'm not allowing you to exercise that faith. So you may decide according to your convictions."

"Thank you, sir. I'd like to go back on patrol with Jesse."

Kramer laughed. "As a Christian, you sure live daringly. Get out of here. Jesse's waiting for you."

Skip left his captain's office and joined Jesse. "Let's go to lunch. I'm starved."

They bounded out the door to their car.

Jesse jumped behind the wheel. "You sure sound happy for a guy who's been targeted twice by an escaped convict and doesn't know if he'll be alive an hour from now." Putting the car in gear, he pulled out into traffic.

"I'm joyful, Jesse, and there's a big difference between joyful and happy. And if the truth is known, nobody knows if they'll be alive an hour from now, because there are no guarantees in life."

"I suppose you have a point there. Now, explain the difference between joyful and happy."

"Happiness depends on outward circumstances while joy comes from within. You can't manufacture joy."

"Then where does it come from?"

"God."

"I should have known you were leading into a religious discussion."

"Hey, you brought up the subject."

Jesse wheeled the cruiser into the parking lot of Becky's Beacon, and they entered the small home-style restaurant that Skip preferred above any other because of their caring and friendly atmosphere. The boys slid into a booth and were immediately joined by a middle aged man in an apron.

"Hey, guys, what do you want?"

"Mike, what are you doing taking orders?" asked Skip.

Mike glanced around his busy restaurant and smiled. "Sharon had to take her baby to the doctor. Carmen called in sick. And Kathy quit an hour ago. So sometimes even the owner puts on an apron and takes orders. Are either of you looking for a part-time job? I'm hiring. You can start today. When does your shift end?"

Skip shook his head. "Sorry, Mike. As much as I could use the extra money, I'm needed more at home."

"How about you Jesse?"

"Are you kidding? Half the department eats in here. I'm not putting on an apron and taking orders from my fellow officers."

"Well, I'm kind of desperate right now, so if you change your minds or if you hear of someone that's looking for a job, send them my way."

"Will do," said Skip. "Incidentally, have you seen the news about the three escaped convicts?"

"Yeah, why?"

"One of them went to prison because of my testimony. Be on the lookout for him. He's in town looking for me, so if anyone unfamiliar stops in asking questions about me, call the police right away."

"You got it. Now, did you guys want to order something, or shall I pull up a chair so we can visit?"

"Funny, Mike," said Jesse. "Give me a double cheeseburger, large fries, and a medium lemonade."

Mike jotted down his order and turned to Skip.

"Grilled chicken salad and an ice tea."

The moment Mike left, Jesse turned to Skip. "How can you be so calm with McKenzie out to kill you? I can't believe how cool you are in the face of such uncertain adversity."

"I didn't realize I was calm. I thought I was agitated."

"Skip, that guy is after you, and I'm a nervous wreck. I can't imagine how rattled I'd be if I were his target. Under the circumstances, you are incredibly cool, calm, and collected. I'd be going in circles like that new father whose baby you just helped deliver. How do you do it?"

"Um...I..." Skip knew that Jesse wanted an answer without listening to him talk about his faith in God, something he couldn't do. He felt at peace due to his relationship with Christ, so how could he elaborate on one without discussing the other?

"Never mind. If this has anything to do with your faith in God, I don't want to hear it."

"Jesse, one day you'll have no choice but to hear it. Only by then, it will be too late."

"What do you mean by that?" demanded Jesse. With a short gasp, he threw up his hand and looked away. "Don't tell me. I don't want to know. Just change the subject."

"Okay. What happened to you on our last radio call? You nearly passed out."

"I don't want to talk about that, either."

"Well, has that ever happened to you before?"

"No."

"Then what happened?" asked Skip. "I had a young woman in labor, a panicked father, a sniper shooting at me from God only knows where, and to top it all off, my partner turned deathly pale and could barely stand up."

Jesse blushed. "That was the first time that I faced the possibility of having to deliver a baby, and I appreciate you bailing me out."

Mike brought a tray with their food and drinks. "Skip, if you change your mind about working here, give me a call. Cause I sure could use someone as reliable and honest as you."

"Hey, I'm reliable and honest," said Jesse.

"Well, since you've already declined my offer, it doesn't matter to me how reliable and honest you are."

Halfway through lunch, Captain Kramer radioed Skip. "Shaun, how soon can you get to the Forest Valley Elementary School?"

"Ten minutes." Abandoning their lunch, Skip and Jesse raced out to their cruiser and took off out of the parking lot with lights and sirens.

Chapter 10

Yesterday's Secret

Skip keyed his mic. "My sisters?"

"They're fine, but a little kindergarten boy named Tommy Stewart crawled into a twenty-foot long culvert. It's plenty big for a kindergartner, but too small for an adult. Between school faculty, his parents, the fire department, and several of our officers, we've been trying to talk him out of there for over an hour."

"He won't come out?"

"No. He's frightened. His teacher said he crawled in there at lunchtime. They've tried every way possible to coax him out before they finally called the fire department. We need someone who might be able to talk him out, and the kindergarten teacher specifically requested I send you."

"We'll do our best, Captain. Our ETA is five minutes."

Skip wasn't prepared for what he saw when they arrived at the school. Emergency vehicles completely blocked both the school entrance and exit. Police cars and fire trucks lined both sides of the street directly in front of the school, and people milled about everywhere.

When Skip and Jesse's unit screeched to a screaming halt down the street from the school, the officers leaped from their cruiser and trotted around by-standers toward the school.

Pacing angrily near the culvert, a tall, muscular-looking man scoffed at the arrival of another police car. "It's a good thing you called for back-up. After all, you're dealing with a wild little five-year-old. It may take six cops and five firefighters to subdue him."

"Be quiet, Thomas," ordered a teary-eyed woman, standing nearby.

Skip suspected that these were Tommy's parents. As he approached, Miss Faye ran to meet him.

"I'm so glad you could come," she said. "Tommy is scared to death that if he crawls out of that culvert, he'll go to jail."

"Where in the world did he get an idea like that?" asked Skip.

"His father, I'm afraid. He's always threatening to have Tommy arrested. From what I understand, this morning when Tommy was getting ready for school, his little sister woke up and wanted out of her crib. Tommy tried to lift her out. Well, she fell and split her lip. Tommy's dad whipped him and said that the police would be waiting for him when he got off the school bus this afternoon. Now you understand why he crawled in there at lunchtime and won't come out."

Skip shook his head. "I can't possibly imagine the fear in that little boy right now. Before he'll come out, he has to trust someone."

"I know. That's why I specifically requested you."

"Is that Tommy's father?" Skip pointed to the man hovering around the end of the culvert with the emergency personnel.

"Yes. His name is Thomas Stewart."

"Where's the rest of your class?"

"The children are inside with the first graders."

Skip glanced around at the school staff and emergency personnel clustered at both ends of the culvert, attempting to coax the boy out.

"And he's been in there for an hour?" asked Skip.

"Yes. He said he's never coming out."

"I'll talk to him," said Skip. "Do me a favor. Please bring Suzi to me."

"Suzi?" Miss Faye raised a questioning eyebrow.

"Yes, ma'am, she can crawl in there. I can't."

Miss Faye nodded knowingly and hurried toward the school building.

Skip turned to his partner. "I need you to clear everyone away from the culvert, including emergency personnel. Then get these people out of here." He motioned toward the growing crowd of curious onlookers.

Kevin anxiously skimmed the crowd for Skip. He'd heard Captain Kramer dispatch him to the school. Not that they needed one more officer there, but if anyone could coax that boy out, Skip could. He had a magical way about him with children.

Thomas Stewart stooped down and yelled into the culvert at his frightened little boy. "Young man, you come out of there this instant, or so help me, when I get my hands on you ..."

"No!" cried Tommy. "I'm never coming out. Never! Never! Never! I'm not going to jail."

Kevin yanked Stewart away from the culvert opening. "We're trying to get him out, not frighten him into taking up permanent residence in there."

Pushing him aside, Kevin squatted beside the opening and called down to Tommy. "Tommy, you're not going to jail. Why don't you come out of there and we'll get you something to eat? I know that you're hungry. Miss Faye said you haven't had lunch."

"I don't believe you. My daddy said that cops always lie to get you to trust them. Then they arrest you and take you to jail."

Kevin looked up at the boy's father, who was standing right beside him. "Did you tell him that?"

"My boy needs to know the truth!" Spinning on his heel, the man stormed away.

Skip jostled his way through the emergency personnel to reach the culvert opening where Kevin squatted.

"Let me try, Kevin."

Kevin stood and stepped aside. "Boy, Skip, I'm glad you're here. If anyone can coax that child out of there, it's you."

Drawing close to Kevin, Skip lowered his voice. "Do me a favor. Clear this area. I don't want that child to see anyone through the culvert opening except me, and I don't want anyone else talking to him, either. Also, don't let Mr. Stewart leave. If necessary, lock him in the cage of your cruiser."

"Gladly. That man's been a menace to our efforts."

Skip dropped to a squatting position at the culvert opening, bowing his head and closing his eyes. *Lord Jesus, please give me the wisdom I need to say the things that will draw that little boy out of there.*

Taking a quick glance around, Skip saw that Kevin and Jesse had effectively cleared the area. Everyone on the scene quieted down as they watched him.

Skip peeked into the culvert and spoke to Tommy. "This is a really small tunnel. "How did you get in there?"

"I crawled."

"Hey, Tommy, are you ready to go for a ride in my police car?"

"No! You'll ride me to jail."

Skip cringed at the panic in his voice. Before Tommy would crawl out of there, he had to trust someone to protect him. And before he could trust anyone, Skip had to calm him.

"Now, why would I do that? You and I are friends. Remember the secret I shared with you yesterday?"

"Yeah."

"Well, I have another secret to tell you. May I come in?"

Tommy laughed. "You won't fit. You're too big."

"I think you're right. Tommy, even though you're in there and I'm out here, we're still friends, aren't we?"

"I don't know."

"Miss Faye told me that you had a rough morning, and I thought you might like to tell me about it." Skip looked up as Suzi joined him.

"I don't want to go to jail." Tommy started to cry.

"Who's threatening to put you in jail? You point him out to me and I'll take care of him for you. I won't let anyone put you in jail."

Skip drew Suzi close to him and whispered in her ear.

"Suzi, crawl down to Tommy and remind him of our secret yesterday, that my uniform doesn't make me a different person. Tell Tommy that I'm still your big brother, and I won't let him go to jail anymore than I would let you go to jail. See if you can get him to trust me enough to come to me."

Suzi nodded.

"Hey, Tommy," called Skip. "Since I can't crawl in there with you, I'm sending a very special person. She has a new secret that I want to share with you. I don't want anyone else to hear it. This is our secret unless you want to share it. Okay?"

"Okay."

"Do you remember what I want you to tell Tommy?" Skip asked Suzi.

Suzi flung her arms around his neck and kissed his smooth cheek. "Yes." Releasing Skip, Suzi crawled into the culvert.

Everything got quiet. Although their voices echoed in the culvert, the children talked too softly for Skip to hear their conversation. And while the others paced anxiously, he prayed for his little sister.

Lord Jesus, speak through Suzi. Use that precious little girl to do something that none of the adults have been able to do – gain that child's trust.

Unable to turn around in the culvert, Suzi backed out the way she'd crawled in. When Skip pulled her out, he saw that Tommy had followed her.

Tommy scrambled out of the culvert into Skip's open arms, embracing him tightly and burying his face in Skip's shirt. Skip lifted Tommy into his arms and stood. Everyone cheered.

Immediately surrounded by people who all wanted the boy turned over to them, Skip grabbed Suzi's hand and pulled her close to him, afraid she'd be knocked down and trampled.

"Tommy." With tears streaking down her cheeks, his mother reached for him.

His head resting on Skip's shoulder, Tommy clung to Skip, refusing to go to her.

"Young man, I want to see you and your parents in my office right now," said the principal. "Do you realize what a fright you gave all of us?"

Several paramedics attempted to relieve Skip of the boy so they could examine him for injury, but Skip refused to release him. Miss Faye jostled her way through the press to reach them.

"Tommy, are you all right?" Taking Suzi's hand, she cocked her head to look Tommy in the face.

The boy wearily nodded.

"Thank you, Miss Faye." Skip ruffled Suzi's blonde hair and sent her with her teacher.

Shoving people aside, Tommy's father barreled through and seized his son's arm. "Thank you, officer. I'll take it from here. I assure you, this little monster will be severely punished."

"Let him go," ordered Skip.

Jesse and Kevin yanked Stewart away from his son. The more that people tried to separate Tommy from Skip, the harder the boy clung to him. Skip knew that he couldn't just release this frightened lad. If they didn't resolve his fears and he didn't feel protected and adequately cared for by the only adult he trusted at this point, the next time, they might not be able to reach him.

"Excuse us," said Skip, stepping away from the others. "Tommy and I need to talk for a minute."

Seeing the child was okay, the crowd gradually dispersed as people returned to their activities. The fire department left and school personnel returned to their classrooms.

Skip carried the child a short distance away, set him on the green grass, and lowered himself to Tommy's eye level.

"Tommy, what happened this morning before school?"

"Are you going to take me to jail?"

"Of course, not. Remember what we talked about yesterday? As a police officer, my first priority is to protect you. Now, tell me what happened this morning. Why did you crawl into the culvert?"

Tears filled Tommy's big brown eyes. "I was helping my baby sister get out of her crib, and she fell on the floor and got hurt. I didn't mean to hurt her. My daddy said that I would go to jail because it's against the law to hurt people."

"Tommy, did your daddy hurt you because of it?"

The child's tender expression glazed over with fear, and his eyes shifted to his father, who stood with Kevin and Jesse by a police car. Skip glanced over at Stewart, glaring at his son with a look that warned him to keep quiet.

Chapter 11

A Growing Concern

Tommy swallowed hard and blinked back tears.

With Stewart standing there, controlling Tommy's every word by his threatening demeanor, Skip turned the boy so he couldn't see his dad.

"Tommy, did your daddy hurt you this morning?" asked Skip again.

When the boy didn't answer, Skip turned him around and pulled up his shirt.

"Hey, you have no right to do that!" hollered Stewart, stomping toward them.

Kevin and Jesse seized his arms and restrained him.

"Sir, where child abuse is suspected, we have every right," said Kevin.

Skip cringed at the unsightly marks that streaked down the boy's back into his britches. Looking up at Kevin, he nodded.

A Score to Settle

Skip watched Tommy. The youngster showed no emotion when Kevin and Jesse handcuffed his dad and seated him in the back seat of a police cruiser.

"I'll book him for you," said Kevin, climbing into his car. "See you at the station." He drove away with his prisoner.

Skip turned the boy to face him. "How often does your daddy whip you like that?"

"Every day. I try hard to be good, but I just can't."

"Tommy, your daddy told you that it's against the law to hurt other people, and he's right."

Tears coursed down Tommy's dirty cheeks. "Am I going to jail for hurting my sister?"

"No, son. That was an accident. We don't arrest children for accidentally hurting one another. But I have to arrest adults who deliberately hurt other adults or children. That's what your dad is doing to you."

"You're 'rresting my dad?"

Skip nodded. "Yesterday, I told you that I arrest people who break the law in order to protect you. Your dad is breaking the law the way he hurts you. Therefore, to protect you, your little sister, and your mother, we have to take your dad to jail."

"What about me?"

"You help your mother take care of your little sister while he's away. And remember, police officers are your friends. We're here to protect you and your family. Come on, if it's all right with your mother, I'll take you home in the police car."

"But school's not over yet."

"I know, but you've had a really long day and need a little rest. Miss Faye will understand. So will your principal."

Standing, Skip grasped Tommy's hand and led him over to his mother.

Breaking free, Tommy bolted into his mother's arms. "Mommy, I'm sorry."

With tear-filled eyes, Mrs. Stewart gathered her young son into a hug. "It's all right, sweetie. I understand. Daddy can no longer keep us apart."

Tommy took his mother's hand. "Skip's driving me home in the police car. Do you want to come?"

Cupping his face in her hands, Mrs. Stewart stroked his tear-streaked cheek. "I can't, baby. Who would bring the car home? But you go home in the police car, and I'll follow you in our car."

By the time Skip and Jesse dropped off Tommy, school was about to dismiss for the afternoon.

"Jesse, we're five minutes from the school. Do you object if we pick up my little sisters since we're already here?"

"Nope."

Returning to the school, the blue and white cruiser coasted to a stop at the curb. Four minutes later, the final school bell sounded, and children poured out of the red brick building. The sight of the patrol car drew instant attention, and Skip's young sisters ran to greet him.

"Skip, why are you still here?" asked Suzi.

Skip opened the back door for the girls. "I stopped by to pick you up."

"Again?" said Sandy.

The girls piled into the back seat, and Skip closed the door. Jumping into the front with Jesse, he turned to Suzi.

"What did you tell Tommy when you were in the culvert?"

"I told him what you said."

"Is that all?"

"No. I promised him that you wouldn't take him to jail, and that you would stop his daddy from hurting him, because you're my big brother."

"Suzi, you're a smart little cookie."

The police cruiser coasted to a stop in front of the house. Skip slid out of the car and opened the back door for his three young sisters. "Play in the house today."

"Aw, Skip." Stephanie gazed into his eyes through his sunshades. "Why do we have to play inside again? It's a nice day."

"I know it is, darling. Please do as I ask."

Stephanie exchanged glances with her two younger sisters. "Okay. But Mom will want to know why."

"Skip?" called his mother from the front door. "What's the problem?"

"No problem. I'll see you later, Mom."

Before she could ask him another question, Skip scrambled into the cruiser, and Jesse took off.

"Skip, when are you going to tell your mother?"

"I intended to tell her after we apprehended McKenzie, but this is the second day since his escape."

"What if we don't catch him soon? You've got to tell her."

Skip gazed absently out the side window. "I know. I guess I'll tell her tonight."

"Does Cassandra know?"

Skip sighed and shook his head.

Returning to Becky's Beacon, Skip and Jesse hurried in to pay for their lunches.

"You guys didn't have to make a special trip out here." Mike rang up their orders at the cash register. "I put the bill on your tab, and you could have paid it the next time you were here."

"Thanks, Mike," said Skip. "That's good to know."

The boys paid their lunch charges and left. Skip couldn't help but notice how Jesse studied him. But then, his cool exterior belied his circumstances. Everyone at the station knew the pressure he was under since Jason McKenzie's prison break, especially Jesse, who'd found himself in the line of fire twice all ready.

And what about his family? Were they safe, or would McKenzie attempt to go after them to get to him? He had to get home as soon as possible. He didn't think that

McKenzie would harm Cassandra, but his mom and sisters could be the man's next target.

Jesse spun the cruiser into a parking spot and Skip leaped from the car before his partner even cut the engine. Entering the station at a hasty trot, he rapped on the captain's open office door.

"Captain, may I leave early today? I'll write my report at home and turn it in tomorrow."

"Go."

"Thanks." Skip dashed down the hallway and into the break room, snatching up the paperwork he needed to complete his last report of the day. Without taking time to change out of his uniform, he headed toward the door, coming within earshot of Kramer's office.

"Captain, can I leave early, too?" asked Morgan.

"Why?"

"You let Skip go."

"That's why you want to leave early? Because I let Skip go? Get back to work." Captain Kramer closed his office door.

Paperwork in hand, Skip pushed through the back door.

Brent sprinted after him. "Shauney, wait up."

"I'm in a hurry, Morgan. What do you want?"

"Don't get smart with me, rookie. My fourteen years of experience with the department could run circles around you. But since you're the captain's pet, you get special favors, like extra time off. Well, I intend to complain about it."

Skip rolled his eyes and shook his head. "Fine, but don't do it in front of my car. I have to leave."

Jumping into his vehicle, he maneuvered around Morgan and sped out of the parking lot, racing across town to get home. Twenty-five minutes later, he spun the car into the driveway and dashed into the house, closing the door behind him.

"Leave it open, son. It's a beautiful day outside."

"I know, but I want it closed."

Trotting down the stairs, Erin paused halfway, hands on her hips.

Skip glanced around the room, looking for his four young sisters. They usually ran to greet him the moment he strolled through the door. "Where are the girls?"

"Cassandra took them to the park. Honestly, Skip, this is the second day that you've picked them up from school, rather than let them ride the bus. It's the second day you've made them promise to stay in the house. It's also the second day that you've come rushing through that door early. Now, will you tell me what's going on?"

"Uh...no." Spinning around, Skip jerked open the front door, but his mother bounded down the stairs and slammed it shut on him.

Skip jumped.

"Come on, son, what's wrong?"

Swallowing hard, he glanced away. "Uh, M-M-Mr. McKenzie escaped from prison."

"Have you told Cassandra?"

Skip shook his head. "No. And I'd sure feel better if the girls stayed inside right now."

"Sweetie, you're the one that's in danger. You were the one he threatened."

"But we don't know his frame of mind, Mom. He might go after the girls."

"That's true. That man was unpredictable. Let's take all the precautions we can."

Without any further prompting, Skip dashed out the door and scrambled into the car. The park was only down the street, but walking the distance would make him an easy target. Coasting to a stop at the curb, he lowered the passenger's window and honked the horn.

"Cassandra," Skip yelled through the open window.

With a big grin, Cassandra trotted over to the car. "Skip, I've got good news. I passed my driving test this morning and got my license."

"That's great, Cassandra. Will you call the girls and get in the car?"

"Why? It's a beautiful day, and we just got here."

"Please, Cassandra. This is important."

Cassandra's smile faded. "Skip, what's wrong?"

"I'll tell you later."

"Um...okay." Cassandra called the girls to the car and motioned for them to climb into the backseat.

"Skip!" gasped Stephanie, crawling into the car beside her younger sisters. "I'm sorry for disobeying you, but Mom wouldn't let us stay inside. Please don't be mad."

Skip winked at her. "I'm not mad, princess."

Cassandra slid in beside him. "Would you like to tell me what this is all about?"

"Later."

"I want to know *now.*"

Skip spoke barely above a whisper. "You'll have to wait. I'm not discussing it within earshot of my little sisters. I'll tell you this evening after they're asleep."

Chapter 12

Going Out After Dark

The girls' bedtime didn't come fast enough for Cassandra, waiting anxiously through supper and halfway into the evening. It was evident that Skip had told Erin, but he wouldn't confide in her. The kitchen was cleaned up. The girls were all in bed. The house was quiet. What was he waiting for?

Cassandra wanted to scream when he sat down at the dining room table with some paperwork from the police department and pulled out his pen. He still had a report to write.

Fine! With a frustrated sigh, Cassandra plunked down on the sofa to watch television.

It didn't take Skip long to write his report, and by now his little sisters should be asleep. He couldn't risk any of them accidentally overhearing the conversation. Slowly rising, he strolled into the living room. This was not something he wanted to do. He jerked to a stop in the doorway.

Oh, boy.

One look at Cassandra told him that he was in big trouble for not telling her sooner. She sat slouched on the sofa with her arms crossed and a scowl marring her pretty face.

It was now or never. Collecting his courage, Skip walked around to Cassandra, picked up the television remote, and flipped off the set.

"Hey! I was watching that."

"I'm sorry. I...I know you were, but I have to talk to you."

"Oh, you finally decided to tell me, huh?"

"No, I decided this afternoon. But I needed to wait for an appropriate time." Skip paused.

"Will you hurry up and tell me. I'm missing the show."

"Cassandra, your father escaped from prison."

"I know. I saw it on the news. Don't worry about it. They'll catch him."

"Don't worry about it? He threatened my life."

"Oh, Skip, my dad would never carry out that kind of threat. He isn't that kind of man."

Skip tensed. This was not going well. "Cassandra, your dad went to prison for killing a cop in cold blood.

That cop was my father. I saw everything. How can you say he isn't that kind of man?"

"Because he isn't."

Skip jumped at the intensity in her voice.

Bounding to her feet, Cassandra paced the living room with clenched fists. "My father is loving, kind, and gentle. He truly loves me, and he wouldn't deliberately hurt anyone. The death of your dad is unfortunate, Skip. My father was wrong to rob that store and kill him, but he didn't go into that store intending to hurt anyone. Your dad walked in unexpectedly and startled him."

Cassandra genuinely believed her father to be a kind and compassionate man, so for Skip to confide in her about the attempts McKenzie had already made on his life would be useless.

Pursing his lips, Skip immediately buried his fear and all emotion under a hard expression that he knew Cassandra would not be able to read.

"Never mind, Cassie. Forget I mentioned it." Skip kissed her and handed her the television remote control. "Sorry for interrupting your program. I'm going to bed."

Cassandra tossed the remote on the coffee table and followed Skip up the stairs. "Is that why you've been picking up your sisters every day?"

"Yes."

Cassandra trailed him down the hallway into the bedroom. "Skip, I'm sorry for yelling at you. But you don't know my dad like I do. I promise, there is no need for you to take precautions against him. He would never intentionally hurt you."

Flipping on the nightstand lamp, Skip quietly closed the door behind them. "Cassandra, it's been years since you've seen him. People change, ya know."

"Yeah, sometimes people change. I just think you're being silly."

Skip grasped her arms and gazed into her big, brown eyes. "Humor me. My precautions won't hurt anything, will they?"

"No, I suppose not. I'm sorry for getting mad."

"Forget it." Cupping her face in his hands, Skip kissed her. "You ready to pray?"

Holding hands, Skip and Cassandra dropped to their knees beside the bed like they did every night. Cassandra squeezed Skip's hand and bowed her head.

"Lord Jesus, I'm sorry for yelling at Skip. Make me patient and kind, like he is. Thank You for saving my mom and my sister. Do whatever is necessary to bring my dad to know You as Savior. Thank you, Lord. In Christ's name, Amen."

"Cassandra, what if God has to take something precious from you before your dad will accept Him. Are you willing to part with anything?"

"Yes," she stated matter-of-factly.

"Even me?"

The next day dragged for Skip as he anticipated another attempt on his life from McKenzie. But his day was quieter than he expected, which unnerved him. Where was McKenzie hiding and when would he strike? Skip knew that it was only a matter of time.

Concerned that McKenzie might target his little sisters, he picked them up from school again and dropped them off at home. Their mother hustled them into the house and closed the door.

Returning to the station, Skip intended to put in some extra hours to make up for the days he left early that week. He knew he wasn't needed on patrol. Captain Kramer had second shift covered, but he likely had some details around the station that needed taken care of, so Skip stopped by his office.

"Shaun, why don't you take off for the day?" said Paul. "You needn't make up the time that I let you go early this week."

"Thanks, Captain."

"And ignore Morgan. He's always griping about something. Nobody even pays him any attention."

Skip breathed a sigh of relief. That was good to hear.

Leaving the station, he detoured to the shooting range for some target practice, firing off several rounds of ammunition. Afterward, he cleaned his gun. It was almost five o'clock when he finally strolled through the front door.

Skip jerked to a stop. The house was unusually quiet. A twinge of fear rippled through him when no one ran to greet him. After all, McKenzie was still running free.

"In here, son," called his mother. "We're eating an early supper."

Quietly closing the front door, Skip locked it with the dead bolt before joining his family in the dining room.

"Hi, Skippy." Suzi's exuberant little voice expressed great delight in his presence, which warmed his heart as much as if she'd greeted him at the door. "Mommy said we had to stay in our seats."

"That's all right, darling. You were a good girl to obey Mommy." Skip sat down beside Cassandra.

"You're late," said Cassandra.

"I went to the shooting range after work."

"Needed to sharpen your shooting skills in case my dad comes after you, huh?"

Exactly, thought Skip, although he did not miss the sarcasm in her voice.

"So do you now feel prepared?"

No.

"Well?" demanded Cassandra. "Are you going to answer me?"

Erin and the girls stopped talking, looking from Cassandra to Skip.

Skip served himself a bowl of beef stew. He didn't really want to talk about this. He had no desire to deal with Cassandra's sarcasm, but he suspected that she wouldn't let it rest until he responded.

"I'm a police officer, Cassandra. It's important for me to maintain my shooting proficiency because I never know when I'll have to draw my gun on the street or when I might be involved in a shootout."

"Oh. Well, that makes sense. I guess it's been quite awhile since you've gone to the shooting range."

Skip prayed and started eating. Cassandra's condescending remarks threw a damper on the relief he felt at finding his family safe, so he ate in silence.

"You're awfully quiet," said Erin. "Did you have a rough day at work?"

"No, ma'am, it was pretty calm."

After supper, Skip sprawled out in the recliner while Suzi and Scooter ran into the fenced-in back yard to swing. Stephanie helped her mother clean up the kitchen, and Cassandra prepared to go out for the evening.

"Skip, I don't feel well." Rubbing her eyes, Sandy climbed into his lap.

Skip felt her cheeks and forehead. "You're running a fever." Embracing his little sister, Skip laid back and closed his eyes. With Sandy nestled in his arms, he drifted to sleep.

A gentle caress tickled him behind the ear. Skip turned his head and felt soft lips brush his cheek.

"Skip, wake up." Cassandra's breath tickled his ear as she kissed him repeatedly.

"Hmm?" Now wide awake, Skip turned his head toward her and opened his eyes. "What is it, Cassandra?"

She caressed his cheek. "Would you please run up to the store for me? I desperately need some hair spray. I didn't realize that I was out."

"Hair spray? You woke me up for that?"

"Please, sweetheart. I have a baby shower to go to."

Skip sat up and lowered the recliner, glancing around the quiet house. "Where is everybody?" He didn't know how long he'd slept, but he must have been really tired, because Sandy had gotten down without waking him.

"The girls are in bed, and your mom is upstairs reading."

Sliding off the recliner, Skip peeked out the window. "Cassandra, it's almost dark outside. Can this wait until tomorrow? I'll pick up hair spray for you on my way home from work."

"I need it now. I'm completely out."

"Borrow some from my mom. She won't mind."

"Please, Skip. I really need my own."

"Why? What's the big deal?"

"Before you and I got married, my mom told me that living with your family might be difficult, and I would make things easier by never borrowing from your mother."

"I'm sure it would be okay just this once," said Skip. "Besides, you look fine. I don't think you even need any hair spray."

"Skip, are you afraid of the dark?"

"Heavens, no."

"Then why are you making up so many excuses to avoid going out?"

"It's an unnecessary trip, Cassandra, and your dad is out there somewhere." *Looking for me,* he thought.

Cassandra heaved an exaggerated sigh. "I see. Never mind, Skip. I'll go myself."

"No, you won't. If you insist on having it tonight, then I'll go get it."

Cassandra's grin declared a victory, while Skip suppressed the fear that she mustn't know he felt.

"Well, would you hurry? I'm late."

"Okay, okay. I'll be right back." Skip relocked the door on his way out to the car.

Wasting no time, he scrambled into the car and locked all the doors. For all he knew, McKenzie had him in his sight at this very moment.

Skip cranked up the car and took off for the nearest grocery store.

Protect me, Lord. Send your angels to go before me, to surround and guard me. I have an uneasy feeling that McKenzie's out there somewhere at this very moment, watching for me, waiting to ambush me.

Skip's senses sharpened as he drove to the supermarket on high alert. He mustn't let McKenzie catch him off guard. The streets were quiet, and traffic was moderately light for that hour of the evening, so the convict likely wasn't tailing him.

Turning into the parking lot, Skip did a broad sweep of the lot. He saw nothing out of the ordinary. Was he overreacting? Of all the locations around town, what were the chances that McKenzie had selected this particular supermarket at this hour of the evening?

Regardless, Skip still parked in an illuminated spot as close as possible to the store. With his gun strapped to his ankle holster under his right trouser pant leg, he scanned the parking lot one last time before leaving his car.

He saw nothing. He heard nothing. He detected nothing. Nevertheless, he picked up his pace, hurrying toward the store. Halfway across the parking lot, his step faltered and he caught his breath at the sound of a gun cocking.

"No sudden moves."

Skip froze. He recognized McKenzie's deep voice, and he was in big trouble.

"Keep moving, kid." McKenzie slammed the heel of his hand between Skip's shoulder blades, thrusting him forward with a hard shove. "Go around to the back of the store and keep your hands in plain sight."

Skip swallowed hard. *Lord?*

Hebrews 9:27 calmed his spirit. *And as it is appointed unto men once to die, but after this the judgment.*

No one misses their appointment with death. *No one!* And everyone has an appointment. Is this his appointed time? If not, he won't be meeting his Maker tonight. If it is, there's nothing he can do to stop it. He just didn't want to die this way.

McKenzie marched Skip to the rear of the store at gunpoint.

"Hands on your head, fingers interlaced."

Trembling, Skip obeyed. He *was* going to die this way, and then Cassandra would regret having sent him out for something so trivial.

"On your knees. I intend to execute you."

Chapter 13

In the Shadows

Panic set in, and Skip froze. His mind raced through all the self-defense moves he'd learned in karate class. He suspected that the moment he threw up the slightest defense, McKenzie would shoot him. But what did he have to lose? One way or another, this man intended to kill him.

"Did you hear me? On your knees. *Now.*" McKenzie poked Skip in the back with his gun.

Skip cross-stepped his right foot behind his left, clenching his fists, and spun around so fast he slammed his right fist into McKenzie's gun hand, sending the gun sailing while slugging him with a left cross.

A mountain of a man, Cassandra's dad staggered backward, momentarily caught off guard, and Skip scrambled for the gun. The instant he grabbed it, McKenzie tackled him, and they both tumbled to the blacktop. Skip hit the pavement hard, McKenzie on top of him, and the gun slipped from his grasp, clattering onto the blacktop. McKenzie belted him and strained to reach the gun.

Despite his karate training, Skip exhausted himself, struggling to keep his assailant from grabbing the gun, which lay inches away. Back-fisting Skip across the face, McKenzie scrambled over top of him and seized the gun.

Skip rolled to his feet and scurried behind some empty boxes. Everything got quiet. But his heart pounded so hard, he could feel it thumping his chest. Listening intently, Skip heard crunching gravel and knew that McKenzie was now on his feet. There were a hundred places to hide. The back of the store was littered with empty boxes, large empty barrels, dumpsters, and piles of lumber.

"Come on, Shaughnessy. If you give yourself up, I'll make this quick and merciful, but I'm not letting you get away. I came here for one reason, and you know what it is."

Skip heard movement and knew that McKenzie was wandering around the back of the store looking for him, so he crept from one hiding place to another. Engulfed in dark shadows, he wiped his sweaty hands on his trousers before withdrawing his gun. His heart thumped harder and louder, but next to his own shallow breathing, silence saturated the stillness surrounding him.

Where was McKenzie? He peeked around some empty cardboard boxes, looking for his assailant. A box toppled over and McKenzie blasted it with two rounds.

Skip hit the dirt, then scrambled to his feet and dived behind some heavy, metal barrels. Gunfire rang out again. A bullet ricocheted off the can, but Skip didn't wait around. He crawled behind the pile of lumber in the corner and crouched low. Heavy footsteps stopped barely two feet from where he was hiding.

Lord Jesus, please don't let him hear or see me, and send backup.

McKenzie walked away. Skip crept around the wooden blockade, searching the darkness for him. Just then, he caught sight of McKenzie's shadowy figure standing in the center of the concrete slab, slowly turning around.

What a relief. He spotted McKenzie before McKenzie located him. Taking careful aim, Skip intended to drop him with a single shot. That's all it would take. One bullet would end this nightmare. He'd rid the world of a convicted cop killer, and wouldn't McKenzie's death be justified? It would be a clear-cut case of self-defense.

Skip swallowed hard. That man wasn't just a felon. He was Cassandra's dad, regardless of the crimes he'd committed. And she loved her dad. If Skip pulled the trigger and killed his father-in-law, his marriage was over. She would never forgive him.

I can't do it, Lord. Skip slowly lowered his gun. *I'd rather die than live with that on my conscience.*

Sirens pierced the silence and McKenzie bolted. The gunshots brought the police, causing him to flee, and he wouldn't return tonight.

With a sigh of relief, Skip dropped to the ground behind the pile of lumber and leaned back against the brick building, exhausted from the overwhelming struggle with his dad's killer. Folding his tired arms across his bent knees, Skip rested his head and closed his eyes. The next thing he knew, a loud voice roused him from sleep.

"Throw down your weapon and come out with your hands up."

At the sound of Tim's voice, Skip wearily looked around. A half dozen flashlight beams illuminated his surroundings, and while several officers surrounded the woodpile, undoubtedly with their weapons drawn, only two of them burst into his corner uninvited.

"Skip!" Tim promptly re-holstered his weapon. He squatted beside Skip and examined him for injury. "Are you okay? What happened?"

"I had a run in with our friendly neighborhood convict."

Standing on either side of him, Tim and Greg lifted him to his feet. Still trembling, his legs weak, he feared his knees might buckle. Fortunately, his fellow officers continued to hold him up.

"Did you shoot at him?" asked Tim.

"No, he shot at me."

"Let me see your gun."

Skip surrendered his weapon. Tim examined it and returned it to him. Re-holstering his gun, Skip staggered. Greg tightened his hold on Skip to keep him from falling.

"Come on, Skip. We'll walk you to your car," said Greg.

Without giving him the opportunity to refuse their help, Greg and Tim supported him on either side as they escorted him out to the parking lot.

"Are you sure you're all right?" asked Greg. "Maybe we should run you to the hospital."

Skip shook his head.

"Then at least let me drive you home. You're pretty shaken."

"Thank you, Greg. I'll be fine."

When Skip reached his car, Tim opened the driver-side car door and seated Skip inside. For his own peace of mind, he glanced in the backseat. It was empty. As the police cruisers left the lot, Skip cranked up the engine of his car and pulled out into traffic. Tim followed him home and lingered at the curb until he entered the house.

"Skip, is that you?" called his mother from the kitchen. With a gasp, she jerked to a stop in the doorway. "Oh, my gosh! Are you all right?" Rushing to him, she pulled him into her arms. "You're trembling. What happened?"

"Did Cassandra leave for the baby shower?"

Erin directed Skip to lie down on the sofa and trotted back into the kitchen, returning a moment later with a warm wash cloth and an ice pack. "Yes, dear. She left quite some time ago."

"Was she angry with me?"

Removing his glasses, Erin gently washed his face before pressing the ice pack to his swollen left eye. "Yes, she was. You took quite a beating. Who were you fighting with?"

"Mr. McKenzie. He cornered me in the supermarket parking lot.

"Did you get the hair spray?"

"No. Do you want me to go back for it?" asked Skip sarcastically.

Erin giggled. "I don't, but what do you plan to tell Cassandra? She was pretty upset that you didn't return right away with what she needed."

"I guess I'll apologize for getting mugged and making her late. What else can I say? I just won't tell her who did it. That will only start another fight. She has no idea what her father is really like."

Seating herself on the sofa beside Skip, Erin held the ice pack and gently massaged his right arm. "I suppose she has never seen that side of him."

Chapter 14

In His Dreams

All the way home from the baby shower, Cassandra grumbled about Skip. How could he be so inconsiderate of her? She didn't ask for much. But she needed her own hair spray so she didn't have to borrow from his mother. Not only did his delay cause her to borrow the hair spray, but it also forced her to borrow a car just to get there. As a result, she was not pleasant company at the shower, and it was entirely his fault.

With a heavy sigh Cassandra turned into the driveway and parked next to Skip's blue Buick. *Well, at least he didn't wreck the car.* Yet, that thought renewed her anger. A car accident would have been a legitimate reason to be delayed, so as far as she was concerned, he had no reason.

Cassandra stormed through the front door. Settled in the recliner, Erin looked up from her Bible. Cassandra's eyes flashed from her weary mother-in-law to her husband, who was sound asleep on the sofa.

"Well, I see that he finally came home." Cassandra threw the dead bolt on the front door and marched over to the sofa, prepared to rudely awaken him before unloading her frustration. With a gasp, she dropped to her knees beside the sofa. "Oh, my gosh! Erin, what happened to him?" Cassandra ran her fingers through his hair and caressed his bruised face.

"He got mugged in the supermarket parking lot."

Tears pooled in Cassandra's eyes as she considered how selfish she'd behaved, never once considering that Skip could actually be in trouble. "Oh, Angel, I'm sorry." Stroking his cheek, Cassandra looked over at Erin. "This is my fault. I insisted that he go. I didn't know this would happen. Was he cornered by a gang?"

"No, dear, just one. But that one was a full-grown, adult male twice his size and strength. All things considered, I think he held his own pretty good."

"Was he mad at me?" asked Cassandra.

"I don't think so. He seemed more concerned that you were angry with him for not returning right away and for coming home empty handed."

"I don't care about the hair spray. I care about him. Oh, Skip. I'm sorry for sending you out after dark for something so trivial." Cassandra gently shook him. "Skip?"

"Let him sleep, dear. He's exhausted."

"He'll sleep better in bed." Cassandra shook him again. "Angel, wake up."

Roused from a sound sleep, Skip felt Cassandra shake him. "Hmm?" Rubbing the sleep from his eyes, he started to sit up. "Is it time to get up all ready?" His body ached with the slightest movement.

"No, sweetie. It's time to go to bed. Come on." Cassandra slid her arm around him and helped him up the stairs.

Ever so slowly, Skip got ready for bed and crawled into her arms. Wrapped in her secure embrace, he drifted back to sleep...

"...Wait here, son. I'll be right back."

Skip's dad stepped from the patrol car onto the deserted sidewalk. With one hand in his pocket, he strolled through the door of the mini market. A shotgun blast penetrated the silence. Skip gasped. Through the large window, he saw his father go down...

"Dad! No!"

...Thrust onto the witness stand, he found himself testifying against his father's murderer again. "You're a liar!" screamed Jason McKenzie. "I'll kill you for that." McKenzie leaped over a table and lunged toward him.

Skip scrambled away, but the powerful man seized his arm and knocked him to the floor.

Skip squirmed and fought to escape.

"You're dead, Shaughnessy!" McKenzie yelled as they hauled him from the courtroom. "If I have to, I'll get my family to do the job!"

"No!" Skip kicked and struggled. Someone was still holding onto him, and he had to get away before McKenzie came after him again.

"*...Come on, Shaughnessy. If you give yourself up, I'll make this quick and merciful, but I'm not letting you get away. I came here for only one reason and you know what it is...*"

"No, please."

"*...I aim to execute you...execute you...execute you...*"

"Skip, wake up! Skip!"

Awakened suddenly, his breathing labored, Skip rolled to his stomach and opened his eyes.

Cassandra heaved a sigh of relief. "Thank goodness, you're awake. I thought I'd never wake you up. Are you all right?"

Skip shook his head, hardly able to breathe, shaking uncontrollably.

"Oh, sweetheart, you're hyperventilating. Come here." Cassandra pulled him into her arms and stroked his hair. "It was just a bad dream, Angel. It's over now. Try to relax and go back to sleep."

Skip snuggled up to Cassandra, unable to stop shaking.

"Do you want to talk about it?" Cassandra embraced him, lightly running her fingers up and down his arm.

"No."

"Did this have anything to do with what happened at the store tonight?" Sliding her hand under his pajama shirt, she rubbed his back.

Skip didn't answer. It had *everything* to do with what happened at the store. As Cassandra caressed him, he started to cool down, breathing easier. Relaxing in her arms, he drifted back to sleep.

The next morning, Skip awoke exhausted, stiff, and sore. Scooting out of Cassandra's arms, he slowly sat up.

"How do you feel, sweetie?" Cassandra caressed him. "That was quite a nightmare you had last night. Do you want to tell me about it now?"

Skip forced a smile. He did, but telling her would start another fight, and he didn't want that. Cassandra idolized her father. To make her understand what he was going through would devastate her.

"Maybe later."

Changing into his uniform, Brent glanced around the deserted locker room. He hadn't felt this good in weeks. He escaped McKenzie's vengeance by driving him toward Shaughnessy. That was cause for celebration. Hopefully, McKenzie took care of Shaughnessy before the police recaptured him. That would eliminate both his problems at the same time. He could only hope.

Brent snapped his padlock on his locker and hurried down the hall to the briefing room, sliding into his seat with a full minute to spare. Skip wasn't there.

"Where's Shaughnessy this morning?"

"Skip's at home recovering from his confrontation with McKenzie," said Jesse.

"McKenzie found him already?" Brent grinned. "How come Shaughnessy didn't bring him in?"

The other officers glared at him.

"What is this? A conspiracy? I just asked a question."

Kevin narrowed his eyes, gazing intently at Brent.

McKenzie must have really caught him off guard if there was a confrontation, and Skip didn't bring him in. How marvelous.

That meant, it was only a matter of time.

Chapter 15

An Unexpected Reunion

With Skip home from work, Cassandra helped her mother-in-law prepare a big breakfast. However, Skip only picked at his food. Cassandra studied him, trying to determine if his lack of appetite was due to extreme fatigue or if he was worried about her father's prison break. She felt certain that his fears were unwarranted, but that didn't ease his concern. Unfortunately, she simply couldn't read him right now. Any apprehension he was experiencing, he kept well hidden from her.

"Angel, are you all right?"

Skip smiled. "Yes, ma'am. I'm just tired. Do you object if I go lie down? I'm really not hungry."

"Not at all. Go get some rest." Cassandra kissed him.

Standing, Skip started to clear his place, but Cassandra placed her hand over top of his. "I'll get it, Angel. You go lie down."

Skip left the dining room and trotted up the stairs.

"I hope he's not coming down sick," said Erin. "He was unusually quiet this morning, and he hardly touched his breakfast."

"I checked for fever when I touched him," said Cassandra. "I suspect he's just tired. He didn't sleep well last night. He had nightmares."

"Nightmares?" Erin's expression glazed over with fear. "What is it, Erin?"

Erin drew in a slow, deep breath. "I'm certain that Skip would prefer you not know. That's why he hasn't told you himself. But the last time he dealt with nightmares, it was during your father's trial, and he experienced them for months afterward."

Cassandra stood and started stacking the breakfast dishes. "He's really afraid of my dad? That's silly."

"Not to Skip. No matter how ridiculous his fear seems to you, the best thing you can do for him is to shower him with your support and understanding. He desperately needs that right now."

Hauling dirty dishes to the sink, Cassandra hurriedly rinsed them and loaded the dishwasher. "Yeah, I guess he does."

Erin washed Scooter's hands and face before lifting her down from the table.

Working together, it took the ladies five minutes to clear and wash the table, load the dishwasher, put away leftovers, and wipe off the counter tops.

"There," said Cassandra. "We're all done. Erin, it's a lovely day. I think I'll walk up to the supermarket and pick up some hair spray while Skip is napping."

Cassandra hurried out the front door and down the sidewalk. Slowing to a saunter, she soaked in the warm, end-of-summer sunshine. As she neared the supermarket, a big, black car pulled alongside her.

A sudden fear shot through her, and she jerked to a stop. Across the street half a block away sat the supermarket, offering her safety and protection within its brick walls. Bolting to the rear of the strange black car, Cassandra glanced both ways and dashed across the street from behind it.

The driver honked his horn and lowered his window. "Cassandra, wait."

"Huh?" Cassandra stumbled to a stop. From the middle of the road, she started back toward the vehicle, now stopped in the middle of the street. "Dad?"

Jason motioned for her to go around the car. "Jump in, sweetheart." Leaning over, he pushed open the passenger's door.

With no further prompting, Cassandra dashed around the car and scrambled in beside her father. The moment she shut the door, he accelerated.

"Dad, I'm glad to see you. Have you seen Mom and Melanie?"

McKenzie shook his head. "I can't get to them. The house is under surveillance. I can't believe I saw you just walking along. What are you doing so far from home?"

"I'm not far from home. I only live down the street."

"You don't live with Mom any more?"

"Nope. I got married."

"Cassandra, that's wonderful. What does Mom think of him?"

"Mom adores him."

"And you live in this upper-class subdivision? Sounds like you'll be well taken care of." McKenzie pulled the car into a motel parking lot and maneuvered it around to the back of the motel, parking in front of the very last room, which looked like it had been long forgotten by the motel because of its location in a right-angle corner. Sliding from the car, Jason motioned for his daughter to follow him.

"Where are we, Dad?"

"My motel room, where we can talk in private." Unlocking the door, McKenzie held it open for her.

Cassandra entered the dimly-lit room. "You know the whole state is looking for you. Everyone says you're dangerous, but I know better than that."

"Of course, you do."

"Where'd you get the car?"

"I borrowed it."

Cassandra cocked her head. "You borrowed it?"

"Well, I didn't get permission from the owner before I borrowed it, but I fully intend to return it. So, tell me, Cassandra. How is my precious little girl? You will never know how badly I've missed you and Melanie." Cassandra's father embraced her.

"I've never been happier. I have the most wonderful husband, and I know Jesus as my Savior."

"What? You got religion now?"

"Not religion. Salvation. There's a big difference."

"Oh, really? And what's that?"

"Jesus said, 'I am the Way, the Truth, and the Life. No man cometh unto the Father but by Me.' Salvation is trusting in God's way to Heaven. God's way is through His Son. But religion is man's attempt to get to God. Man can't get to God. If he could, then God would have had no need to send His Son."

"Cassandra, is your husband a preacher?"

Cassandra started laughing. "No."

"I'm glad to hear that. I don't know how long I could tolerate this nonsense."

"It's not nonsense. You need to trust Jesus as your Savior, too. I don't want you to die and go to hell."

"Does your mother know that you've turned religious?"

"I haven't turned religious. I already told you. I got saved."

"Well, whatever. Does she know about it?"

"Yes. Mom and Melanie have gotten saved, too. If only you'd get saved, Dad."

"That's not for me, Cassandra. Even if I believed in God, which I don't, He wouldn't want anything to do with a loser like me. Now, tell me about your husband. He must be a real winner if your mother likes him."

"Oh, he is, Dad. He's the handsomest, dreamiest, sweetest guy in the world."

"Cassandra, how long have you been married?"

"Three months. Why?"

"Because it's obvious the honeymoon hasn't worn off yet."

"Dad, I wish you knew him. He's like you in so many ways. He's really strong, but he's also kind and compassionate, gentle and loving, a real gentleman. He always opens the door for me."

"What does he do for a living?"

"He's in law enforcement."

McKenzie raised an eyebrow. "You're kidding! Cassie, does he know his father-in-law is a convict?"

"Yeah, he knows."

"And he married you anyway?"

"Dad!" Cassandra threw a pillow at him.

"I'm sorry, princess. I'm glad you're so happy."

"I am. But with my husband in law enforcement, I tend to worry about him. If anything happens to him, I'll die of a broken heart."

"Well, I'm sure he'll be all right."

"Daddy, if you haven't been by to see Mom and Melanie since you've escaped from prison, what brought you to Forest Valley?"

Jason cleared his throat and his expression turned hard. "I have some unfinished business here." His voice sounded bitter.

"What kind of business?"

Her father tensed, pursed his lips tightly, and stared into space. Turning to Cassandra, he smiled, all evidence of anger and hostility replaced by a soft disposition. "Never mind, princess. Don't concern yourself with it."

"All right. I've got to go now. I'll stop by again tomorrow."

"You wouldn't turn me into the police, would you, darling?"

"Certainly not. But one thing bothers me. Since you're a convict at large, you have no legitimate means of income. How are you surviving?"

"Well, um ..." McKenzie looked away.

"That's what I thought. You're stealing. Here, Dad." Cassandra emptied her purse and folded some bills into her father's hand.

"No, Cassandra. I can't take this. What would your husband say?"

"He's a God-honoring Christian, Dad. He'll understand. But please don't steal."

"You're sure this won't upset him?"

"Positive. Now take it. I've got to run." Cassandra kissed her father's cheek and hurried outside into the bright sunlight.

Her father was staying at the motel just on the other side of the supermarket. How wonderful. She lived walking distance from his motel room. She would definitely plan to visit him again soon.

Without a doubt, Brent had directed McKenzie to the right part of town, so the moment Cassandra left, he started plotting his next attack. This time, Shaughnessy wouldn't escape.

Chapter 16

The Element of Surprise

Skip lay awake in bed trying to shut out his worries and trust in God's ability to protect him. He bordered exhaustion, but he couldn't sleep. Every time he closed his eyes, he saw McKenzie coming after him. He dreaded the man's next attack, and he feared for his family's safety. If God didn't intervene, he would soon be joining his father in Heaven.

Bolting upright in bed, he grabbed his Bible. *Lord, what am I thinking? You've already intervened, or I wouldn't even be here. Look at how many times he's shot at me. Hebrews 9:27 says that everyone has an appointment with death. My mom, each of my little sisters, and, of course, me. And You would never let an escaped convict rush us to any of our appointments. That's in Your hands.*

Skip opened his Bible. It was time to hear from God. *And I have got to pull myself together. How can I function effectively on the street or protect my family if I'm falling apart. Lord, please help me to let go of my continual worry and to trust You completely.*

After praying for God's perpetual protection on him and his family, Skip turned to the Psalms and started reading, meditating on each passage of Scripture. As he read his Bible, God's peace warmed him like nothing else could. But he still craved Cassandra's tender support. And that was something he didn't seem to have access to.

As his eyes grew heavy, Skip lay down, his Bible open on his chest, and he dozed. When he awoke, he felt so rested, he thought he must have slept for two hours, but according to the clock, he hadn't even been in his room for a full hour, so he couldn't have slept more than twenty or thirty minutes.

Skip closed his Bible and set it on the nightstand. Crawling off the bed, he adjusted his clothes, smoothed a few wrinkles in his shirt, and headed down the stairs. Scooter leaped up from the floor where she colored a picture and ran to greet him.

"'Kip! 'Kip!"

Skip snatched her up and swung her into his arms. "Hi, Scooter Pie." He kissed her baby soft cheek, and she threw her arms around his neck, hugging him tightly.

Erin looked up from the recliner, where she sat reading her Bible. "Well, you look refreshed. Have a good nap?"

"Yes, ma'am, thank you." Skip glanced around the quiet house. "Where's Cassandra?"

"She went for a walk."

"By herself?"

"She'll be all right. Mr. McKenzie won't harm his daughter."

"Yeah, you're right." Skip set down his little sister and sent her to play. Snatching up the newspaper, he sat down to read, constantly watching for Cassandra's return. Twenty minutes later, the front door opened, and Skip bounded to his feet.

"Where did you go?"

"Well, I started to go to the store, but I didn't make it. I'll go tomorrow. Skip, can I have some money?"

"I just gave you thirty dollars. What did you do with it?"

"I gave it away."

"You what?"

Stepping over to him, Cassandra slid her arms around his neck and drew him into a kiss. "I gave it away. On my way to the store, I met a man in need. I gave it to him so he wouldn't have to steal to eat. So now I'm broke."

Skip gazed into her warm, compassionate eyes. "Cassandra, I'm not made of money, ya know."

Cassandra kissed him again. "I know, Skip, but he really needed it. And I still need hairspray."

"Tomorrow I'll stop after work and pick it up for you."

"Absolutely not!"

Skip drew back at her tone of voice. "Cassandra, don't raise your voice with me."

"After what happened to you last night, I don't want you anywhere near the supermarket."

"Well, I'll make a note of it and tell dispatch I'm not allowed near that supermarket, so if anything goes down there, they'll have to send another officer to take the report."

Cassandra noticeably relaxed. "Thanks, Skip. Now, if you'll give me some money, I'll run over there tomorrow and pick it up."

Skip raised an eyebrow. He was being facetious, and she took him to mean exactly what he said. Should he tell her that he had no intentions of avoiding that supermarket while on duty?

"Cassandra, I have to drive right by the supermarket on my way home from work. Wouldn't you like me to stop by tomorrow and save you a trip?"

"No, that's okay. You don't know what kind I use, anyway."

Skip sighed. "All right." He pulled a twenty-dollar bill out of his wallet and handed it to her. There went his lunch money.

"Thanks, Skip." Cassandra kissed him and ran to put it away.

Relaxed on the sofa at the end of a busy day, Erin studied the newspaper crossword puzzle. Her family was fed, the kitchen cleaned up, lunches made for tomorrow, and her daughters ready for bed. Still sick, Sandy was already in bed for the night. Scooter and Suzi watched cartoons on television before bedtime, and the last time she saw Stephanie, her daughter was sitting at the dining room table drawing.

"Have you heard from Aunt Rose?" Skip asked his mother. "I was just wondering."

Erin looked up from her crossword puzzle, but before she could answer Skip's question, her ten-year-old daughter approached.

"Mom, I don't feel well." Stephanie sat down beside her mother.

"Not you, too." Setting aside her pen and newspaper, Erin cupped Stephanie's flush face in her hands, feeling for fever. "You're coming down with what Sandy has. Let's get you to bed."

The next morning, Erin bounded out of bed before daylight. She spent time in prayer and in her Bible before rousing Suzi for school and Skip for work. While Suzi was eating breakfast, Erin checked on Sandy and Stephanie. Their fevers had risen over night, so she woke them both to take some children's Tylenol. Coming out of their bedroom, she ran into Skip in the hallway.

"Bye, Mom, see you after work." He kissed her cheek. Jacket in hand, he trotted down the stairs and out the front door.

Staring after him, her hands on her hips, Cassandra heaved a frustrated sigh. "He should not have gone to work today. He's got a black eye. And he's got to be sore. Why didn't you let him sleep in, Erin?"

"Because he's scheduled to work today, Cassandra, and he asked me to wake him when I got Suzi up for school. Besides, a black eye is not a legitimate reason to call off. Now, after I get Suzi on the bus, you and I will sit down to a nice breakfast while the girls are still sleeping."

Cassandra smiled. "I'd like that."

The morning flew by. And while Erin's day was consumed with the care of her two sick daughters, Cassandra straightened the house and occupied Scooter. Shortly before noon, they all sat down to lunch.

Erin drooped into her chair. She was ready for a nap. Maybe she could lie down with Scooter this afternoon.

Cassandra hurried through her lunch. "Erin, I'm going for a walk." Rising from the table, she cleared her place and pushed in her chair. "I'll stop by the store while I'm out and pick up my hairspray. Do you need anything?"

"No, dear, but thanks for asking."

"Well, don't worry about the dishes. I'll do them when I get back." Cassandra kissed Scooter and hustled out the door with a bounce in her step, making Erin wonder what she found so exciting about walking up to the store for hairspray.

Carrying Scooter up the stairs, Erin tucked her sleepy four-year-old into bed for a mid-day nap. Quietly, she slipped into the bedroom of her two eldest daughters. Stephanie and Sandy were also asleep. Erin brushed her hand against their flush cheeks.

"Well, at least Sandy's fever has finally broken." Just then, the phone rang. Erin hurried down the hall to her bedroom and grabbed the phone. "Hello?"

"Mrs. Shaughnessy, this is the nurse at the Forest Valley Elementary School. Suzi's running a fever."

"Oh, no." Erin groaned. "I'm sorry. I'll have to call her older brother at work to see if he can get away. There's absolutely no way that I can get to the school right now."

Skip and Jesse were on their way to lunch when the call came over their police radio for Skip to phone home. Jesse pulled into the nearest service station and Skip phoned his mom.

"Sweetheart, I'm sorry to bother you at work, but the school called. Suzi's sick. Can you swing by the school and pick her up for me? Cassandra went to the store and I can't leave the girls."

"Sure, Mom, no problem. See you in a little bit."

Bryan Brady and his younger brother, Kenny, relaxed under a big, shade tree at the park across the street from the elementary school. With hardly a cloud in the sky, a warm breeze rustled the trees that surrounded them.

"Nice day to be free, isn't it?" said Bryan.

"For us." Kenny fiddled with the tuning knob on his transistor radio. "I wonder where McKenzie's hiding out. We've searched this entire town."

Chewing on a blade of grass, Bryan nodded. "He's doing a good job of keeping a low profile. That's for sure."

The radio crackled and Kenny turned up the volume to catch the rest of the news report on their brother. "...from prison last week. One convict was shot during the escape. He's listed in stable condition. The other three convicts are still at large. Be advised, they are armed and dangerous."

Kenny flipped off his radio. "Well, Roy's still holding on. If only we had a way to get him out of there."

A police car pulled up to the curb at the driveway directly in front of the school, and Bryan grinned when two police officers stepped from the cruiser. "Maybe there is, Kenny."

The two officers closed their car doors and trotted into the school building.

Bryan grinned.

"You got an idea?" asked Kenny.

"Yeah. Let's engineer a prisoner exchange program."

Kenny's eyes widened. "How in the world do we pull it off?"

"We'll kidnap a couple cops and trade them for Roy's release."

"You're joking. Right?"

Bryan glanced around the quiet community. "No. It ought to be easy. Not a soul anywhere."

Kenny glanced around the park. Then he looked up and down the street in front of the school. "Hey, you're right."

Bryan bounded to his feet. "This will be a cinch. Let's go."

Brushing off their clothes, the Brady brothers crossed the street and strolled nonchalantly toward the cruiser. They made small talk, slowing their pace while waiting for their kidnap victims. A moment later, the two officers exited the school building and strode toward their car with a little girl between them. One cop opened the back door for the child while the other officer strolled around to the driver's side, keys in hand.

Reaching the patrol car, Bryan and Kenny separated. Knowing that a gunshot would draw attention, Bryan decided to overpower and disarm the cop with the element of surprise. He seized the driver's wrist, attempting to twist his arm behind his back, but the officer yanked free and jerked his gun out of his holster. Diving for his arm, Bryan knocked him to the street.

"Skip!"

Chapter 17

A Prayer for Deliverance

Kenny stepped directly behind the blond cop who was busy securing the youngster's seat belt. At the sound of his partner's distressed call, he looked up.

"No sudden moves, and no one will get hurt." Kenny cocked his gun and tried to relieve the lad of his weapon, but he couldn't free it from the holster. "Just keep your hands where I can see them."

"Skip!"

Grabbing Skip's handcuffs off his belt, Kenny locked his wrists together behind his back, pushed him into the cage of the police car with the little girl, and closed the door.

"Having troubles, Bryan?" Kenny strolled around the car.

His brother lay sprawled on top of the cop, wrestling him for the gun, so Kenny stepped on his wrist.

"Release the gun or I'll break your wrist."

The moment the officer loosened his grip, Kenny snatched up the police-issue, 40 Caliber Glock, while Bryan jerked him onto his stomach and slammed him into his own handcuffs.

"Let's get out of here before someone sees what's going on."

Lifting the cop to his feet, Bryan and Kenny shoved him into the cage of the cruiser and slammed the door. Bryan located the car keys from where they'd fallen during the scuffle, and he jumped behind the wheel of the police car. His brother hopped in beside him and they took off.

Bryan drove around the park to the isolated area where they'd left their sister's car parked, and he pulled up beside it. Climbing out of the cruiser, the Brady brothers yanked open the back doors.

"This one's trouble," said Bryan. He jerked the troublesome cop out of the police vehicle and dragged him to the back of his sister's car. Bryan opened the trunk, shoved him in, and slammed it shut.

Kenny stared at his brother in disbelief. He hadn't realized that Bryan had become that hardened. "What about this little girl? We can't leave her here. She saw everything."

"Ah, bring her along. So we have three hostages, instead of two. More bargaining power that way."

Skip glanced from one abductor to the other. These men weren't common criminals. They were escaped convicts.

Great! He and Jesse had led little Suzi right into this mess. They should have been alert and paying attention, knowing that McKenzie and the Brady brothers were on the loose. He was as good as dead now. Skip suspected that McKenzie and the Brady brothers were good friends. After all, they escaped prison together, and these men would undoubtedly turn him over to Jason McKenzie, who would likely kill both him and Jesse. And what would become of his five-year-old sister? Would they kill her, too?

Oh, Lord, are we in trouble, thought Skip. He frantically glanced around for the curious sight-seers and on-lookers who were easily drawn to emergency vehicles of any kind. But there wasn't one person in sight.

Kenny Brady pulled open Skip's car door and grasped his arm. Jerking him from the car, Kenny marched him over to a red Taurus and forced him into the back seat, making him move into the middle. Reaching around him, Kenny secured his seatbelt and pulled it tight.

"Don't waste your time buckling him in. He's not worth the effort."

"In my book, he is. His hands are cuffed behind his back. If he's wearing a seatbelt, he's locked down, and there's no way he'll get out of the car by himself."

"Oh, good point."

Kenny pulled Skip's crying little sister from the cruiser and shut the door. He led her over to the Taurus. She willingly climbed into the car next to Skip and snuggled up to him. With tears trickling down her flush cheeks, she clung to his arm.

"Please don't do this to my brother."

Kenny slammed her back against the seat and buckled her seatbelt.

"Leave her alone!" ordered Skip.

"Young lady, you're sitting right beside him, now stay in that seat belt." Kenny looked at Skip. "And you're not in any position to be giving orders. So unless you want to be gagged, shut up." Snatching off his glasses, Kenny dropped them into Suzi's lap before blindfolding him.

Crying softly, Suzi looped her arm through Skip's and rested her head against him. "Skip, I want to go home. I don't feel good."

"I know you don't, sweetheart." Her face felt feverish as her hot tears trickled down his arm.

The drive was unbearably long and uncomfortable. Skip expected the Brady brothers to talk while they drove. At least, that's what normal people did. He hoped to glean some informational tidbits from their conversation that could be useful later, anything that might tell him what road they were on or which direction they were headed. He'd overheard Bryan say that they could use Suzi for more bargaining power. Bargaining power for what? Their freedom? But they didn't discuss anything, not even the weather. So with the quiet rumble of the engine and the sound of the tires on the blacktop, Suzi slumped against him, sound asleep.

And the blindfold left Skip feeling incredibly alone with nothing but his thoughts. He couldn't escape the vivid images of Bryan Brady forcing his good friend into the trunk of the car.

Lord, I'm scared. What do they plan to do with us? Send an angel to go before us, to guard and protect us, but especially Jesse. He's not ready to go out into eternity. Suzi and I would go to be with You, but he'd go to hell.

Skip's arms ached and his wrists throbbed, but when the car finally rolled to a stop on a gravel surface, he started trembling.

Bryan yanked open the car door. Reaching around the sleeping child, he unsnapped her seatbelt and lifted her from the car, passing her to his brother. Kenny lifted her into his arms and carried her into the house. Bryan unbuckled Skip's seatbelt and jerked him out of the car. Still blindfolded, Skip tripped and stumbled as Bryan dragged him up the walk and shoved him through the front door.

Appearing at the top of the stairs, Ariel Brady frowned. Because of the twelve-year age gap between him and his baby sister, Bryan naturally assumed control of her home and her life when he arrived on her doorstep a few days ago.

"Well, it's about time you got home with my car." Ariel gasped.

For a moment, she stood dumbfounded and speechless at the sight of Bryan's hostages. Skipping down the steps, she dashed over to them and scooped the child out of Kenny's arms.

"Did they hurt you?" Ariel smoothed back her long, blonde hair. "Oh, my. You're running a fever."

"I'm so tired." The little girl rested her head on Ariel's shoulder.

"Aren't you guys in enough trouble all ready? No! You won't be satisfied until I go to jail, too. Well, I want no part of this."

"Too late, Ariel. You're all ready part of this," said Bryan. "Take care of that kid. Then meet us in the basement with the video camera. We're making movies."

"Get out of my house!"

Bryan grinned. "Our house now, little sister. You see this young cop in handcuffs?"

Ariel looked at Skip. "Yeah."

"Well, his partner's locked in the trunk of the car."

"You're not serious!"

"I am. And our hostages will go with us. Trust me, they won't live to tell what we'll do to them."

Ariel clutched the small child and studied the blindfolded cop. Even Bryan thought that the lad appeared remarkably calm, considering his circumstances, but then, what choice had they given him?

"Bryan, you wouldn't! Not this innocent child."

Ah-ha! Ariel's greatest weakness. "Especially that innocent child."

Licking her lips, Ariel glanced from her brothers to Skip. "All right, you may stay, providing you promise not to harm this little girl."

Bryan crinkled his nose. "Take her, Ariel. We wanted these two cops, anyway."

"And you won't hurt either of those police officers, will you?"

"Not if they co-operate. Does that satisfy you?"

"No, but I suppose it's better than nothing." Spinning around, she trotted up the stairs with the child in her arms.

"What does she expect us to do? Leave Roy in prison?" said Bryan.

Grasping Skip's arms, Bryan and Kenny marched him up the stairs and into the first bedroom on the left. The small, cream-colored room contained a solid wooden dresser and a four-foot by six-foot sturdy wire cage bolted to the hardwood floor. A large curtainless window filled the room with sunlight. Bryan had intended to throw a soft mattress down on the cage floor for his sister, but he didn't care if Skip slept on a hardwood floor.

After stripping the kid's uniform of his radio and gun belt, Bryan removed the handcuffs and shoved him inside. The lad tumbled to the solid wooden floor, and Kenny secured the door with a metal padlock.

"Behave yourself, boy, and we won't have to put these back on you," said Bryan. He and Kenny strolled out the door, closing it behind them.

Skip slowly removed the blindfold. The sudden brightness gave him an instant headache. Almost immediately, he slapped his hand over his eyes. Slowly sitting up, he peeked through his fingers and looked around. Except for his homemade jail cell and a small dresser, the room was empty. Folding his hands, he bowed his head to pray.

"Heavenly Father, I'm scared, more for Suzi and Jesse, than myself. Please take care of Suzi. Send angels to surround and protect her from harm." Skip choked down a lump as he continued. "And safeguard Jesse. Lord, you know why I don't talk to him about you. But I love him like a brother and pray every day that he'll come to know you as his Savior. He's not ready to die. Please protect him, Lord, and send your angels to deliver us, like you did for Peter."

Chapter 18

A Change in Uniform

Jesse's arms ached, and his wrists throbbed from the clenching of the handcuffs. And boy did he hurt from lying on all that equipment attached to his belt.

The car finally stopped moving. He'd heard car doors slamming and knew that everyone had gotten out of the car. Hopefully, someone would open the trunk and let him out soon. It was warm and stuffy inside, in addition to cramped. He tried to stretch his legs a little, but there was no place to move them.

Lying quietly, Jesse listened intently, but he heard no voices or movement outside the car. The Brady brothers must have dragged Skip and Suzi off somewhere and left him locked in the trunk. What if they never let him out and he died in there? Not wanting to dwell on that thought, Jesse closed his eyes, but the minute he did, he saw fire.

Although that frightening vision startled him, and he opened his eyes, his cramped prison was still quiet and dark. Jesse had never felt so alone in his entire life. They were all going to die today, and he wasn't ready to die. Why didn't he allow Skip to share his faith when he had the chance? Then at least he'd know what he needed to do to be saved, because he might never see his best friend alive again. And the words he'd recently exchanged with Skip came back to haunt him…

"…Says who, church boy? You claim to trust in God. Where was He when we were almost killed an hour ago?"

Oh, Skip, I'm sorry.

"Oh, were you blaming God? Here I thought you were mocking my faith. What was I thinking?"

Jesse choked back hot tears. He *was* mocking Skip's faith.

"…Never mind. If this has anything to do with your faith in God, I don't want to hear it."

"Jesse, one day you'll have no choice but hear it. Only by then, it will be too late."

"What do you mean by that?" demanded Jesse. With a short gasp, he threw up his hand and looked away. *"Don't tell me. I don't want to know. Just change the subject."*

How he wished that Skip had told him anyway. Now, he wanted to know. He needed to know. And Skip wasn't there to tell him.

He heard a key being inserted into the lock, and the trunk popped open, flooding the trunk with sunlight. Jesse squeezed his eyes shut just as strong hands grasped his arms and pulled him from the car.

Bryan Brady shoved a tightly clenched fist in his face. "If you try anything, I'll bury you in the backyard. It's a cop like you that shot my brother!"

Clasping his arms, the Brady brothers dragged him into the house. With his eyes still adjusting to the light, Jesse found it difficult to see where he was going. Nevertheless, he attempted to take note of his surroundings, watching for Skip or Suzi as they forced him through the basement door and down the steps.

Bryan pulled the light cord at the bottom of the stairs, filling the underground storage room with light. Kenny unlocked the handcuffs and shoved Jesse into the center of the room. He floundered and sprawled to the concrete floor on his stomach, falling on his equipment-laden police belt. He hit the floor so hard, he smacked his head and got the wind knocked out of him.

"Get up!" said Bryan. "We want that uniform! You got two minutes to take it off!"

Stiff and sore from his long, cramped car ride, hardly able to move, Jesse struggled to his feet.

"Hurry up!" Bryan kicked his feet out from under him and knocked him to the floor again. "You got one minute left."

Jesse mustered together all his strength and picked himself up off the floor. He glanced uneasily from Bryan to Kenny and back to Bryan. He saw no guns, although that didn't mean they weren't packing. He had to assume they were both armed. But one thing was certain, they had *his* gun.

Jesse glared at them. "Where are Skip and Suzi?"

Kenny kicked him behind the knee, buckling his legs. Twisting his arm behind his back, Kenny jerked him to his feet and Bryan repeatedly slugged him.

"Stop it!" A young woman bounded down the stairs. "Leave him alone, Bryan! You promised."

"I said they'd have nothing to worry about if they co-operated. This one refuses to co-operate." Clenching his fist, he slugged Jesse again.

"Here! Here's the camera! Now let him go." The girl thrust a video camera into Bryan's hands and pushed him away from Jesse. "Let him go, Kenny. Now!"

With an angry glare, Kenny shoved Jesse into her arms and stomped away. Jesse pulled away from her. Holding his head, he slowly sat down on the floor, his knees bent. The beautiful young woman knelt beside him, cupping his chin and raising his head as she studied his face. Jesse glanced up at his abductors, who paced back and forth.

Rising to her feet, the girl stepped between Jesse and his captors. "Bryan, don't hit him again."

"That depends on him." Bryan glanced at his watch and looked at Jesse. "You've got one minute."

"One minute for what?" asked the girl.

Jesse knew, and he had no desire to get beat up again. He dropped his gun belt, removed his radio, and stripped off his police uniform. At the moment, he didn't even care that the girl was in the room.

Bryan grinned. "Kenny, get our guest something special to wear for our movie."

A moment later, Kenny handed Jesse a prison uniform. "Put it on."

Jesse slipped into the orange jumpsuit. Stamped across the back was the word 'Inmate.'

"Fits him good. Doesn't it, Bryan?"

"I'll say. It fits him perfect."

Bryan looked through the eyepiece of the small video camera. "We intend to film you, your partner, and that little girl to send to the Forest Valley PD so they will know that you've all been kidnapped."

That meant Skip and Suzi were still alive. Jesse breathed a sigh of relief.

"Ariel, grab his uniform and go upstairs to check on that child," said Bryan.

"She's sleeping. She wasn't feeling well."

"That's all right. Go check on her anyway."

Ariel eyed her brothers suspiciously before hurrying up the stairs.

Jesse caught his breath. He suddenly felt quite vulnerable.

The instant the basement door closed, Kenny and Bryan seized his arms and slammed him back against a heavy metal grill that was bolted to the floor near the far wall. Wrapping rope around his wrists, they threaded it through the grill and securely bound him to it.

"You're a troublemaker," said Bryan.

Stepping back, he turned on the video camera, filming Jesse in his present condition. While recording him, Bryan narrated what else they would do to him if their brother wasn't released within forty-eight hours. When they finished, they pulled the light cord and hustled up the stairs, closing the door and leaving him in darkness.

Skip jumped when the Brady brothers barged in with an orange jumpsuit.

Ariel hastened into the room after them. "Bryan, Kenny." She stumbled to a stop, her mouth wide open at the sight of the large cage. "So this is what you two were up here building. Where's your other prisoner?"

"It's none of your business, Ariel. What do you want, anyway?" said Kenny.

"That child is really sick. I think we need to get her to a doctor."

"No!" shouted her brothers.

"She's running a high fever and crying for Skip."

Skip leaped up. "That's me. Please, let me go to her."

"No," said Bryan. "You're not going anywhere. Now, get out of that uniform. You have one minute."

Seeing Ariel watching him, Skip slowly unzipped his shirt. He unwillingly undressed in front of her.

Bryan unbuckled his belt and yanked it out of the belt loops. "You exceeded your time limit. Kenny, unlock his cell door."

Ariel grasped Bryan's hand. "Don't touch him. He co-operated. That was our agreement."

Bryan glared at Skip. "Hand me your clothes, kid." After trading uniforms with Skip, he turned to Ariel. "He's not permitted to leave this cell. But you may bring that little kid in here."

"I knew you had a little heart under that rough facade."

Ariel dashed from the room, returning a minute later with Suzi in her arms. Kenny opened the cage door for her, and Bryan pulled a gun.

"Don't try anything heroic. I'd hate to see that child get hurt," said Bryan.

Skip zipped up the orange jumpsuit and reached for Suzi.

"Skip, take me home."

Skip lifted her into his strong arms, embracing her. "I can't, sweetheart. You and I are prisoners right now. We can't go home."

While Skip talked to Suzi, Bryan videotaped them.

"I want Mommy."

Skip sighed. "You and me both, kid-o."

"Where's Jesse?"

"I don't know."

Resting her head on Skip's shoulder, Suzi snuggled up to him.

"Okay, kid. Visiting hours are over." Bryan motioned with his gun. "Get the kid, and get out of there, Ariel."

Ariel stepped out of the cage and closed the door. "Why? Let her stay with him. It won't hurt anything."

Bryan stomped his foot. "Ariel, would you like to take over?"

"I'd love to. I'd start by releasing your hostages."

"What?" cried Kenny. "What about Roy?"

"He's in prison for murder! He deserves to be there! And so do you!"

Bryan slapped his sister across the face, knocking her to the floor. "Ariel, don't you ever talk to me that way! Now, get that kid, and get her back to bed."

Ariel glared at him. Getting to her feet, she stepped into Skip's prison cell and lifted Suzi out of his arms. Skip reluctantly let her go.

"Skip!" Crying and clinging to him, Suzi refused to go to Ariel. "Skip!"

Skip squeezed his eyes shut and looked away, attempting to tune out the cries of his little sister. Ariel finally wrenched her away from him. It took every ounce of his strength to let her go without a fight, and as Ariel left the room with her, he could hear her screaming all the way down the hall.

Chapter 19

Ariel's Intervention

Ariel thought Suzi would never settle down, and she feared what her brothers might do to the child if her constant crying agitated them. So she rushed the little girl into her bedroom and closed the door. Settling in her rocking chair, she attempted to soothe the hysterical child, whose fever was rising due to her persistent squalling.

"I want Skip."

Suzi cried so hard, Ariel had difficulty consoling her. "Shh, baby, I know." Ariel gently rocked her.

Fortunately, her brothers would be gone awhile, delivering that video to the police department, and the moment they got home, they'd turn on the ballgame. That gave her time to quiet Suzi. Ariel held her for nearly an hour before she finally quit crying.

A Score to Settle

Humming softly, she rocked Suzi until her breathing was steady and she felt limp. Ariel breathed a soft sigh. The little one had fallen asleep. Standing with the child in her arms, she stepped over to the bed and gently laid her down. Suzi never stirred.

Ariel brushed her hair off her face. "You poor thing. You don't belong here. Neither does your sweet brother. I'll bet your mother is beside herself with worry over you two."

Leaving her uncovered, Ariel slipped into the hallway and softly shut the door behind her. Heading toward the stairs, she paused outside the closed bedroom door where her brothers held Skip prisoner, keeping him isolated. She didn't dare open that door. But the padlock securing their prison was one of hers, and she had a spare key for it.

Ariel passed by his room and continued on down the stairs to make supper. She wondered how much longer her brothers would be gone while contemplating her predicament. She lived out in the country, far from the nearest town. Her brothers had cut her telephone lines and taken her car keys. At the risk of what they might do to her, she had to help their hostages escape.

Trotting into the kitchen, she rummaged through a drawer of miscellaneous items, searching for her spare key. If she found it quickly, she could help the two police officers escape before Bryan and Kenny returned.

"Where is that thing?"

The front door burst open and her brothers noisily entered.

There it is. Ariel pocketed the key.

With her house full of people, Ariel prepared a big supper, only to discover that Bryan had no intentions of letting her feed his prisoners.

"That does it, Bryan! I demand you treat those officers with kindness. They're hungry, too."

"Ask me if I care. Now, get in the kitchen and fix my plate."

"Fix it yourself! Either, you let me feed them, or I quit."

Bryan jammed his hands in his pockets and glared at his sister. She had him over a barrel, and he knew it. He could keep her prisoner here, but he didn't possess the power to make her cook and clean for them.

"Ah, go ahead and baby them, but you serve us first." Spinning on his heel, he stormed off.

Forced to be servant and maid, Ariel resentfully served her brothers before checking on Suzi and taking a tray to Skip. The moment she entered his room, his eyes grew wide.

"Dinner! I missed lunch, so I'm starving."

Ariel set his plate on the floor and slid it under the wire door. Then she slid a bottle of water through one of the wire squares.

"Thank you." Skip picked up his plate. "How's my sister?"

"She's sleeping."

"Where's Jesse? Is he all right?"

Ariel frowned. "I don't know. He was last time I saw him, but that was hours ago. How come he's not up here with you?" Rising quickly, Ariel trotted down to the basement, flipping on the light.

"Jesse?" She stepped around the corner and jerked to a stop. Jesse's weary body drooped against his restraints.

Sprinting over to him, Ariel freed his wrists and promptly ducked under his arm. With his arm around her neck, and her arm around his waist, she helped him up the basement steps. Although the basement was cool, Jesse's skin was warm to the touch.

"Is Skip all right?" he asked her.

"Yes. He's upstairs."

"And Suzi?"

"She's sleeping."

Pushing open the basement door, Ariel glanced uncertainly at her brothers, who sat on the sofa watching a ballgame. If they didn't stop her, she would take Jesse upstairs to be with Skip. At least that way, they'd have each other for company and support.

Bryan and Kenny gaped at her as she guided Jesse through the downstairs and up to the second floor. Leaping up, Kenny dashed after them.

Ariel pushed open the door to Skip's room. "Leave him alone, Kenny. He needs to lie down."

"No problem. He can lie down on this nice hardwood floor." Kenny unlocked the cage door and shoved Jesse inside. Jesse lost his balance and tumbled onto Skip.

Snapping the padlock back on the door, he strode from the room.

Skip scooted out from under his partner and helped Jesse sit up. "Oh, my gosh! What did they do to you?"

Jesse glanced around the room. "Skip, where's Suzi?"

"Ariel's taking care of her."

Jesse looked up at the girl.

"I'll bring you some dinner."

Ariel hurried down the stairs and into the kitchen, preparing Jesse a plate of food. She watched her brothers intently. They were so wrapped up in that ballgame, they seemed oblivious to her. When she took Jesse his supper, she could give him the key to the lock. Bryan and Kenny would never know.

But what if they suspected her of plotting against them? They knew her sympathies lay with those two police officers, not with two escaped convicts, who illegally took possession of her home and car and forced her into servitude, regardless of their relation to her. That might cause them to search their prisoners before going to bed.

If Bryan found the key on one of those officers, there was no telling what he would do to them. But she felt certain that he wouldn't search her, so she'd slip them the key after her brothers had retired for the night.

Chapter 20

The Topic of Conversation

"Kidnapped!" cried Paul. "How can two armed police officers with a five-year-old child in their custody get abducted in broad daylight? Somebody must have seen something."

"We checked all ready, Captain," said Johnny. "Kevin and I have banged on a hundred doors within a two-block radius of the school and the park where we found their car. We even went into the school and grilled the faculty. We asked everybody. Nobody saw anything."

Paul sighed. "I guess we can change our missing person's reports to reported kidnappings. I've already notified Jesse's wife, but how do I tell Skip's mother that, not one, but *two* of her children were abducted?"

"You haven't told Erin, yet?" gasped Johnny.

Paul shook his head. "No. I sent an officer out to her home, but no one answered the door."

"I'll run out there," said Johnny.

"Did you see the tape?" asked Kevin. "They're wearing orange jumpsuits."

Paul nodded. "Yeah, I saw it. They want Roy Brady released in forty eight hours or their three hostages are dead."

"Didn't Brady get shot during a prison escape with three other inmates?" asked Johnny.

"That's right. Two of those inmates were his younger brothers. The third, Jason McKenzie, has threatened Skip and wants him dead. Even if we succumb to their demands, they'll likely kill Skip anyway."

The other officers exchanged sober glances.

"So now what?" asked Kevin. "Where do we even begin a search?"

"Maybe they're staying with a relative," said Johnny.

Kevin's mouth dropped open. "Brady is a really common name. It would take days to check them all."

"We don't have days," said Paul. "We have less than forty-eight hours. So you'd better get started. Since Skip and Jesse are wearing prison uniforms, these convicts have possession of their police uniforms and may try to pass themselves off as cops. Do a background search of the Brady brothers and McKenzie. Check out every possibility. We have to find them before it's too late."

"Yes, sir," said Kevin.

"I'm gonna run out to Erin's home to let her know what's going on," said Johnny. "Then I'll be back to help you, Kevin."

Standing in the kitchen, the phone to her ear, Erin laughed at the amusing story Rose had just shared with her.

She had been on the phone with Rose for almost an hour now. How she wished she had a cordless phone. It would've been nice to kick back in her recliner while enjoying the conversation with her new best friend.

Rose was right in the middle of her story when Erin's doorbell rang. Not that she wanted to answer it. It was likely a door-to-door salesman, but she didn't want the doorbell to wake her sleeping daughters.

Speaking of sleeping daughters, where was Suzi? She thought Skip should have been home by now with his little sister.

"Well, Erin, despite the hilarity of the situation, I got everything taken care of for my company. The moving company is coming on Wednesday, and it will take them two days to get everything packed up. Then they will load everything into the semi on Friday. So I booked our flight home for Saturday afternoon. If it's all right, we'll be with you folks through the weekend, and the movers should deliver our household goods on Monday."

"Rose, you and the boys are always welcome here."

Just then, Erin's doorbell rang again.

"Well, I got to go. That door-to-door salesman who keeps ringing my bell is persistent, and I don't want it to wake the girls."

"We'll see you on Saturday," said Rose.

Erin hung up and hurried to the door, swinging it open. She caught her breath at the sight of Johnny standing at her door in uniform.

"Oh, no," said Erin. Before Johnny could reply, tears welled up in her eyes. "Where are Skip and Suzi?"

Leaving the store, Cassandra strolled into the bright sunlight with her grocery bag containing hair spray and two giant-sized candy bars – one for herself and one for her dad. It was such a great day for a walk that she turned toward her dad's motel, in no hurry to get home. When she finally reached his room, she rapped on the door.

The curtains ruffled and someone peeked out the window. A moment later, the door swung open and her dad greeted her with a smile. "Hello, Princess, come in."

"Hi, Dad. I had to run to the store, and since I was so close, I thought I'd pop in."

"I'm glad you did. Have a seat."

Cassandra sat down on the edge of the bed and pulled the two candy bars from her grocery bag, handing one to her dad.

Jason took the bar and ripped off the wrapper, chomping down. "Thanks, Cassandra. I haven't had a

Snickers bar in years. So what did your husband say when you came home broke?"

Cassandra tore into her candy bar and took a bite. "He told me that he wasn't made of money, and he gave me the last bill out of his wallet. Poor thing. He didn't have any lunch money today. I wouldn't have taken it, except his partner is very generous."

McKenzie raised an eyebrow. "He didn't get mad?"

"Nope. In fact, I don't think I've ever seen him angry. He's really sweet, Dad, and he's so patient. He taught me how to drive a car, a standard transmission."

"Really? And he kept his cool the whole time?"

Cassandra nodded. "He's different from any guy I've ever met, Dad. You've got to meet him."

"I'd like to. And Mom approved of him?"

"Oh, yeah, Mom adores him. Dad, why don't you come to church with us on Sunday?" asked Cassandra. "Then you can meet him."

McKenzie burst into laughter. "Show up in public? No way. No offense, dear, but don't forget, I'm still a fugitive. It's important for me to keep a low profile. Besides, if he's in law enforcement, he'll be looking for me. You haven't told him where I'm hiding, have you?"

Popping the last bit of candy into her mouth, Cassandra shook her head

"Good girl. I knew I could count on you. Don't fret, dear. I'll meet him as soon as I finish an unpleasant task."

"Okay, Dad. I have to go. But before I leave, I want to give you something." Cassandra handed her father a pocket New Testament.

"What's this?"

"It's the little Bible that my husband gave me when we were dating. This Book is precious to me for two reasons. It was a gift from my husband, and my salvation was a gift from Jesus. And I want you to have it. You are precious to me, and in this little Bible you will find forgiveness and eternal life." Cassandra placed it in his hand and kissed his rough cheek.

Jason sat on the bed at a loss for words. After his daughter left, he glanced down at the small Book in his hand.

"A Bible. Ain't that cute." He tossed it on the end table next to his bed and picked up his stolen binoculars, scanning the parking lot of the supermarket across the street.

Jason smiled as he studied cars coming and going, as well as the people. *He should be here soon.*

Chapter 21

A Matter of Perspective

Setting aside his dinner plate, Skip examined his partner. "Are you sure you're all right? You look horrible."

"I'm all right. They beat me up for not co-operating. I'm just sore."

The bedroom door opened, and Ariel entered with a tray, setting it on the floor in front of their prison door.

"Sorry it took me so long." She slid Jesse's plate of food under the door and passed him a fork, a bottle of water, and napkins through one of the wire squares. "I'll be back later to collect the dishes."

Without waiting for a response, she left their room and closed the door tightly.

"We have got to get out of here," said Skip. "And we're escaping tonight while they're sleeping and it's dark."

Jesse picked up his plate and started eating. "How?"

"I don't know, yet, but I've already..." Filling his mouth with food, Skip stopped himself before he used the six-letter "p" word.

"You've already what?"

Prayed. And I'm relying on God to help us escape.

Skip sidestepped his question. "We're getting out of here. And by the time they realize we're gone, we'll be too far away for them to find us."

"I'm scared, Skip."

"I am, too, but I'm not going down without a fight."

"What about your kid sister? She still has her whole life ahead of her."

Skip heard what Jesse didn't say. *I'm afraid to die.* Studying his friend, he recalled their first day as partners.

Grasping Skip's hand, Jesse said, "I heard you graduated number one in your class. Good for you. I also understand that you're religious. Well, I'm not, so don't ever bring it up around me. That's the quickest way for us to become enemies. Do we have an understanding, Skip?"

Skip gazed into Jesse's serious eyes. "Yeah, Jesse, we have an understanding."

Skip looked away, wondering if he should even attempt to discuss with Jesse his need for a Savior. No doubt, they were in a serious situation with no guarantee of another day. And it was obvious to Skip that Jesse was considering this. So if he was ever going to bring up the subject, it was now. He may not have another opportunity. Skip said a brief prayer in his heart, asking God for wisdom and the right words.

"Don't worry about Suzi. God's watching over her at this very moment, and He'll take care of her."

Jesse stopped eating and looked up at Skip. "What about us?"

"We're good friends, Jesse. I love you like a brother, but don't you really mean, 'What about me? I'm not ready to die.'" Skip studied his partner, trying to read Jesse's expression to know if he should continue or drop the subject.

"And you are?" Jesse resumed eating.

"Well, yes and no."

"What do you mean by that?"

"I don't want to die any more than you do. So, no, I'm not ready to die, but I'm prepared to die. One day, all of us will face death. Death is certain. And when that time comes, I know beyond all doubt that I will go to Heaven."

"How can anyone know for certain?"

Skip studied his partner curiously, allowing him plenty of opportunity to end their discussion, but Jesse's eager-to-know expression prompted him to continue. "The Bible tells us. The book of First John says, 'And these things have I written that ye may know that ye have eternal life.'"

"Does it really say that?"

Skip slowly nodded, surprised by Jesse's sudden burst of excitement.

"How can *I* know?"

After praying for his partner every night for over two years, Skip found himself at a loss for words. He couldn't believe what he just heard.

"First, you must realize that you're a sinner and that you can't save yourself. The Bible says 'For all have sinned and come short of the glory of God.'"

"But I try hard to do what's right."

Skip smiled. "So do I, but that's not good enough to get into Heaven. God requires perfection. Sin can't enter Heaven, and we're sinners by nature."

"Then if sin can't get into Heaven, and we're all sinners, how do we get there?" asked Jesse.

"Romans 6:23 says 'The wages of sin is death, but the gift of God is eternal life through Jesus Christ our Lord.' God requires payment for our sin, so He sent His Son to pay the penalty. It's God's gift to all mankind. And all we have to do is accept His gift by believing on His Son, Jesus. Acts 16:31 says, 'Believe on the Lord Jesus Christ and thou shalt be saved.'"

"That's all I have to do? Believe?"

"And turn from your sin."

"Well, I try to do that anyway," said Jesse. "I told you, I always try to do what's right."

"Romans 10:13 says, 'For whosoever shall call upon the name of the Lord, shall be saved.' Do you want to pray with me, Jesse? Do you want to ask Jesus into your life so that you'll go to Heaven when you die?"

"Yes." Bowing his head and folding his hands, Jesse talked to God. He confessed that he was a sinner. Then he asked Jesus to come into his heart and save him.

Jesse looked up expectantly. "I don't feel any different. Did anything happen?"

"Yes, you just received the most precious gift known to mankind, and God recorded your name in the Lamb's Book of Life. You won't feel any different. Salvation is by faith, not feeling. Just know that God is not a liar nor Indian giver, and you can safely trust in His promise of eternal life."

"That's a relief. Well, Skip, I'm not ready to die, either, but at least now I'm prepared. And I owe you an apology for the way I've acted lately. I know a great deal of it has to do with my background, but that's still no excuse."

Skip glanced toward the window. The sun was going down, and the room was starting to get dark. "I take it, you had a bad experience as a kid."

"That's the understatement of the year. I'm the youngest of five boys, and my family was very religious. Serving God was important as long as it didn't interfere with the bar on Saturday night or gambling or hunting out of season or even stealing. We never missed church, and while my parents drilled me on the Ten Commandments, insisting I keep them all and be a model child, my older brothers used to make me crawl through cellar windows and unlock businesses because I was the smallest and could easily get in. My parents knew what was going on. But as long as we weren't caught, they looked the other way."

"Oh, my. I had no idea you'd come from such a background. Is that why you chose law enforcement?"

"It is. My brothers bullied me a lot, and even into my adolescence they pushed me into illegal activities. So they were thrilled when I joined the police academy."

"Really? How about your parents?"

"They were upset. They wanted me to go into the ministry, like my brothers."

Skip gasped. "Your brothers went into the ministry?"

Jesse nodded. "That didn't change them. They still tried to control me through threats and intimidation, especially after I joined the police force. They figured that I could use my badge and authority as a cop to bail them out of trouble. But when I didn't, they started preaching at me about quitting my sinful job and joining them in the ministry. I didn't want anything to do with their hypocrisy or their so-called religion. But I've always had a burning desire to know God and how I could get to Heaven."

"Boy, that explains a lot."

"I'm sorry for the things I said to you, Skip. My hostility had nothing to do with you, or God, for that matter. But all my life, religion was crammed down my throat by the ungodly, and I wanted nothing more to do with religion of any kind."

"Well, Christianity is not a religion. It's a way of life. Being religious doesn't make you righteous. It doesn't sound like your family knows the Savior."

"They don't, but I've been watching you, Skip. You're a *real* Christian."

"When a person has a close relationship with Jesus, it comes through in everything they do. That's why I couldn't discuss certain topics without referring to God. You might say, God is my partner through life. Just like you and I. When we get out of this situation, will you be able to share it with anyone without talking about me?"

"Why would I want to? You and I are in this thing together, and I know that if we get out of it, we'll do it together, not by ourselves."

"Exactly. Well, that's how I view my relationship with Jesus. I cannot consider the recent attempts made on our lives without thanking Him for protecting us, just like He's doing at this very moment."

"You weren't beat up or forced to ride in the trunk of the car."

"That's true. Ariel stopped them from beating me."

Jesse sighed. "Come to think of it, she intervened on my behalf, too."

"We're both still alive," said Skip. "And we were fed a decent meal. Something tells me that Ariel made sure we ate, not her brothers."

"I guess it's all a matter of perspective."

Chapter 22

One Step Closer

Finishing their supper, the boys stacked their plates and slid them under their cell door for Ariel. Then they guzzled their water.

"Boy, was I thirsty," said Jesse. "Where are we, Skip?"

Skip shook his head. "I haven't the slightest idea. They blindfolded me."

"Then how will we know which way to run if we manage to escape?"

"That's a good question, Jesse, and I don't know the answer."

Hardly able to keep his eyes open, Jesse lay down on the floor and fell asleep.

Skip folded his trembling hands and bowed his head to pray. "Lord Jesus, thank you for bringing Jesse to know You as Savior. Thank you for guarding and protecting us. Thank you for sending your angels to surround Suzi. And thank you for making a way for us to escape. Please send a host of angels to encircle and protect us, and guide us to safety."

Rising to his feet, Skip stepped carefully around his sleeping partner and rattled the door to their prison. It was almost too dark to see. He tugged on the lock and examined the cage for any weak links, especially at the door hinges. He'd thoroughly examined it once before, but he hoped that he'd missed something the first time. He did not. It was constructed very soundly. The only way that he could envision breaking out of this cell would be with wire cutters, and unfortunately, he didn't have any on him. Not that he could see what he was doing.

With a frustrated sigh, Skip dropped to the floor and sprawled out beside his partner. Positioning his hands behind his head, Skip rested his foot on his bent knee and stared angrily at the ceiling. Angry at the Brady brothers for putting him into this position and angry at himself for allowing it to happen.

We've got to get out of here. Skip pursed his lips in deep thought. His mind raced as he considered every possible avenue of escape. With a disheartened sigh, he realized that he had no avenues. Not one.

That means it's up to you, Lord. You're going to have to open the door yourself, just like you did for Peter.

Skip glanced at his wristwatch. It was almost eleven, two hours past his bedtime, and he was exhausted enough to fall asleep right there beside Jesse. But if he did, when God opened their prison door, he might miss his one and only chance of escape. Suzi and Jesse depended on him.

Just then, the bedroom door opened. Ariel stepped into the dark room with a bright flashlight, and she quietly shut the door. Skip looked over at her.

"Hi." Ariel spoke softly. "I wanted to say goodnight. Bryan and Kenny went to bed a few minutes ago, and I'm turning in now." Kneeling outside the cage near Skip, she reached through the wire and grasped his hand, placing a small metal object in his palm.

Skip's heart raced. *A key!* God just opened their prison door.

Then she slid the flashlight through a wire square and handed it to him. "Take this. You'll need it." Pursing her lips, Ariel touched Jesse's cheek and rested her hand on his forehead. "He's running a fever. I fear he might be coming down sick like Suzi."

"How is Suzi?" Skip scooted over to Ariel and grasped the wires.

"She's still very sick. When you go out that door, make a left. She's in the first room on the right. Take the blanket with you. In fact..." Ariel paused, resting her hand on Jesse's head again. "I'll leave you one for him. You're going to need it. And good luck, Skip."

Skip reached through the wire squares and grasped her hand. "Come with us."

Ariel shook her head. "I don't dare. I'd better stay to buy you guys as much time as possible."

"You're a brave girl."

"I'm a scared girl. Send the police as soon as you're able. Right now, I'm almost as much a prisoner as you." Squeezing Skip's hand, Ariel rose to her feet. "Good luck, Skip." She left the room and softly closed the door.

Skip flipped off the flashlight to conserve the batteries.

Peering through binoculars, Jason grinned when he spotted a patrol car pulling into the parking lot of the supermarket.

"There he is." Jason tossed the binoculars on the bed and stepped out the door into the night. He dashed across the parking lot to intercept Brent Morgan.

Brent jumped from his cruiser and shut the door. Jason slipped up behind him with a gun, listening to him ramble.

"This is incredible. The store manager called me, Brent Morgan, to say that I'd won a hundred dollars worth of merchandise. First the home entertainment center and now this. Boy, will my wife be surprised."

Jason rolled his eyes. Morgan didn't recognize his voice on the telephone and fell for the ploy that brought him racing to the store, one he and his wife have probably never even shopped at. But he was too greedy to consider those little details.

With a quick two-step, Jason shoved the barrel of the handgun into the small of his back. "Don't move,

Morgan. Keep your hands where I can see them at all times."

Brent froze.

"Hand me your gun."

Slowly withdrawing his weapon, Brent handed it back to Jason.

Slipping the small handgun into his pocket, he kept Morgan covered with his own gun. "Now get back into the police car and drive."

"Look, Jason, you don't want to do this." Brent jumped behind the wheel of the car, and Jason slid into the passenger's seat beside him.

"I owe you, and since I've been convicted of murder before, it won't bother me to repay you with a bullet from your own gun." Jason directed Brent to drive the cruiser behind the motel where he was staying.

Morgan parked the car and cut the ignition. "Are you going to kill me?"

"Shut up, and I might let you live. Now get out of the car."

Morgan stepped from the cruiser with his hands above his head and the car key in his right hand. Jason snatched the key from him and marched him into the motel room at gunpoint. Brent slowly backed up to the wall.

Jason grinned. "This will work out nicely. Your uniform ought to fit me fine. Take it off!"

Brent stood frozen to his spot, his eyes wide with fear, but Jason pointed the Glock at his head.

"Never mind. One bullet between your eyes will take care of you and not ruin my uniform."

"No! Don't!" Brent dropped his gun belt and radio. Unzipping his shirt, he started to undress. "Here. Take it."

Jason held the gun loosely, watching him strip off his uniform. "Turn around!" Jason jerked his arms behind his back and locked him in his own handcuffs. "Now sit down on the floor!"

Morgan backed into the wall and slid down to the floor. "What are you going to do with me?"

Jason caught sight of the small New Testament lying on the end table. As if drawn by a magnet, he felt compelled to pick it up. Ignoring his prisoner, he sat down on the bed and reached for it. Jason opened the front cover and read the inscription.

"To my darling, precious Cassandra. Words can not express my love for you. Neither can they reveal the infinite love that the Savior has for you. Read and cherish the words of this precious Book. Never part from them. For in them, you will find eternal life." And it was signed, "SS."

What a beautiful message this boy wrote to his daughter. Jason felt touched by the love and warmth from the lad's heart as it radiated off the page. He read it again, truly pleased that his beloved daughter had found such a caring and tender mate, one that would, no doubt, bring her years of happiness.

Carefully opening the Bible, he lay down to read. It was almost midnight before he realized how late it was.

"Jason, I'm sorry for everything. I'll give you anything you want to make it up to you."

Anger pierced his heart and he bolted upright. "That's impossible. How can you possibly give me back the last six years of my life? And the first two were all your doing. You got me hooked on drugs. Drugs that plunged me deep into debt, destroyed my family, caused me to steal, and finally led me to murder to feed my habit. Morgan, there's only one person I despise more than you right now. That's the bratty kid who testified against me and sent me to prison four years ago. I want his address and phone number."

"I don't have them."

Jason kicked off his tennis shoes. "If you value your life, you'll get them."

"Why are you coming to me?"

Changing into the police uniform, he slipped the New Testament into his hip pocket. "Cause you're the only traitor I've come across. That boy has a lot of friends, and no one else will betray him." He pulled on his shoes, hoping no one noticed that his shoes didn't quite go with the uniform.

"What's the number to the police station? Being a fellow officer, you'll be able to get that information." Jason dialed the number and held the phone to Brent's ear. "Watch what you say."

"Hi, Tammy, this is Brent. It's after eleven. I can't believe you're still there...Yeah, you don't normally work that late. Hey, listen, while I got you, could I get Shaughnessy's phone number and address?" His eyes widened and he caught his breath. "He's been what?" He listened attentively. "Yeah, thanks for the information. Bye."

Jason trembled in anger when Morgan ended the conversation without obtaining the information he wanted. He slammed down the receiver. "I ought to kill you right now."

Morgan looked up at him. "Shaughnessy's not home. The Brady brothers grabbed him, and they will only release him in exchange for Roy Brady. That's why the dispatcher was still there. She was helping officers run down information on his possible whereabouts."

"Then Kenny and Bryan have him." Jason snatched up some rope and tied together Brent's legs. Then he slipped the rope between his handcuffed wrists and anchored him to a heavy chair. "See you later, pal." Slapping a heavy piece of tape over his mouth, Jason flipped off the light on his way out the door.

Chapter 23

A Run for Freedom

Curled up on his left side, the flashlight in his right hand, Skip rested his head on his folded arm. He wanted to give the Brady brothers time to drop into a sound sleep before attempting an escape. But if he fell asleep, as tired as he was, he feared he might sleep all night. Yet, he knew that if he got a little rest now, it would greatly increase their chance of escape.

"Lord, if I fall asleep, would you wake me about one."

Skip's eyes popped open. Rubbing the sleep from his eyes, he sat up and looked at his watch. Almost one o'clock. It was time to run.

"Thanks for the sleep, Lord, and for waking me. Help us get out of here without detection, and get away safely."

Pulling the key from his pocket and flipping on the flashlight, Skip quietly unlocked their cell door before rousing his partner. Skip gently shook him and whispered in his ear. "Jesse, wake up. Let's get out of here."

Jesse's arm felt so hot that Skip brushed his hand against his partner's forehead when he sat up. "Just great. You're burning up."

"Yeah, I don't feel very well. Did you say we're getting out of here?"

"Right now." Skip lifted Jesse to his feet. "Let's go." He removed the padlock from their cell door and pushed it open.

Jesse caught his breath. "How'd you do that and where did you get the flashlight?"

"Ariel gave it to me, along with the key for the lock." Skip turned off the flashlight and handed it to Jesse. "I don't want the light to wake anyone. Now, do you know the quickest way out of the house? I was dragged through this place blindfolded."

"What about your kid sister?"

"We're going to get her right now."

"Do you know where she is?"

"Yeah." Skip guided his partner through the bedroom door and down the hall to the first bedroom on the right. The door was ajar. That meant he could get in and out without a sound. Leaving Jesse in the hallway, Skip slipped into Ariel's bedroom. His little sister lay beside her, sound asleep.

Skip cringed. Despite his circumstances, he felt like he was violating Ariel's privacy, creeping around her bedroom in the middle of the night while she was sleeping. But he had no choice if he wanted to rescue his little sister.

Skip wrapped Suzi in the blanket on which she slept and lifted her into his arms. Suzi snuggled up to him, resting her head on his shoulder. As he turned to leave the room, he caught sight of a folded blanket on the armchair with Suzi's shoes sitting on top of it.

Oh, good. Ariel left Suzi's shoes handy and a warm blanket for Jesse, thought Skip. He grabbed them on his way out the door.

Skip left the door ajar, like he'd found it, and rejoined Jesse in the hallway. The house was so dark that he didn't know which way to go. He remembered climbing stairs, but which direction took them back to the stairs? The Brady brothers were sleeping up here somewhere, so they couldn't afford to wander the wrong way and risk waking one of them. How he wished he'd thought to ask Ariel for directions to the front door.

"Jesse? Which way do we go?" he whispered.

"Um..." Jesse looked up and down the hallway. "This way."

He led Skip back the way they'd come, sliding his hand along the wall. They passed the room where they'd been held prisoner, and Skip quietly closed the door all the way, like the Bradys had it.

Skip bumped into Jesse, unable to see that he'd stopped. "Why'd you stop?"

"We're at the stairs. I didn't want you to fall."

Sliding his foot forward, Skip felt the edge and reached for the handrail. Holding Suzi with one arm, Skip slid his right hand down the polished banister as he carefully descended the stairs.

Halfway down the stairs, Skip's heart nearly stopped when he heard a bedroom door open upstairs, followed by light footsteps in the hallway. He and Jesse froze. As softly as they walked, their boots still left the sound of muffled steps. With a front yard security light illuminating the downstairs with a soft glow, Skip was no longer blinded by the darkness.

"Maybe it's Ariel," whispered Jesse, so softly Skip almost didn't hear him.

Skip shook his head, responding just as softly. "I left Ariel's door ajar. We wouldn't have heard it open."

A light flickered on upstairs, followed by the sound of a bathroom fan, and a door clicked shut.

"Go. Go. Go," said Skip. Boy was he glad they'd turned off the flashlight. That bright beam in a dark room would have been like a neon sign.

Jesse moved quickly and quietly. Skip slipped down the stairs after him, moving as silently as possible. The moment his foot touched the floor, the bathroom door opened upstairs and the hallway light flickered on. The boys darted opposite directions just as one of the Brady brothers started down the stairs. One of Suzi's shoes slipped from his hand, and Skip had no time to pick it up. He ducked out of sight, praying that his little sister made no noise in her sleep and the little shoe didn't give them away.

Holding Suzi tightly, Skip glanced around for Jesse, but he was nowhere to be seen. He peeked around the corner and cringed when he saw his sister's shoe lying on its side beside the stairs.

Kenny trotted down the stairs into the kitchen and the light flickered on. Skip heard him rummage through the cupboard and open the refrigerator door. A moment later, the refrigerator door closed.

"Mmm, that was good," said Kenny. "Nothing like a nice cold glass of milk at bedtime. Maybe now, I'll go to sleep." He switched off the kitchen light, and trotted back up the stairs. A moment later, the upstairs hallway light flickered off, leaving them in near darkness.

Skip rose from his hiding place. With an insomniac convict upstairs, it was a miracle that they weren't caught. Jesse rounded the corner of the stairs and scooped up Suzi's shoe. The boys headed for the front door, slipping out quietly and locking it behind them. A cool, brisk breeze greeted them, and they shivered in short sleeves.

Jesse heaved a sigh of relief. "Oh, my gosh. I thought we'd never get out of there."

"Well, we're far from safe standing on the front porch," said Skip. "We've got to put some distance between us and them, and we've got to do it fast."

Without waiting for a reply, Skip handed Jesse the blanket and headed for the road. "Here, Jesse. Wrap it around you."

"You stole a blanket?"

"Certainly not. Ariel left it for us."

Jesse pulled the warm blanket around him. "Aren't you cold?"

Skip shivered. "I'm fine."

Jason thought he remembered the directions to Bryan's sister's house, but he had an incredibly difficult time finding it. He missed his turn and got lost big time. Bryan said it was hard to find, but this was ridiculous. He finally found it and parked Morgan's police cruiser in her driveway.

"Kenny. Bryan. Wake up and let me in." Jason hammered the door with his fist.

Bryan finally opened the door, rubbing the sleep from his eyes. He jumped at the sight of the uniform.

"Relax, Bryan. It's me." Jason brushed past him and entered the house.

"Man, Jason. Have you any idea what time it is?"

"Yeah, it's almost three a.m. Where is he, Bryan?"

Bryan shook his head and quietly closed the door. "Where's who?"

"Shaughnessy. You've got him. Where is he?"

"Who's Shaughnessy? I haven't any idea what you're talking about."

"Bryan, where's the police officer you kidnapped?"

"Well, I kidnapped two of them, and they're both upstairs. Why?"

"Because I have unfinished business with one of them."

"Can't it wait till morning? I'm tired."

"No."

Bryan yawned. "Well, if you insist, I'll take you to them. I don't care if they get any sleep. All I ask is that you leave me one of those cops in semi-decent condition to trade for Roy's release. They won't do me any good if they're both dead. Also, whatever you do, do it quietly so you don't wake Ariel, or I'll never hear the end of it."

The men sprinted up the stairs and into the first bedroom, flipping on the light. The cage was empty and the door stood open. Spinning around, Bryan dashed down the hall into the next bedroom. Jason followed him.

"All right, Ariel. They're gone. *Start talking.*"

"Gone?" Ariel looked down at the bed and gasped. Leaping out of bed, she shoved past her brother and dashed down the hall, flinging open the door. "How did they get away?"

Jason and Bryan exchanged glances.

Bryan clenched his fists in anger. "You know how. You helped them, so you might as well admit it."

"I didn't." Ariel retreated.

"Yes, you did." Seizing his sister's wrist, Bryan dragged her to the cage and flung her in. Ariel tumbled to the floor and her brother snapped the padlock on the door. "I'm not giving you a chance to take off. We originally built this thing for you, anyway."

"No. Bryan, don't do this to me. *Bryan!*"

Bryan flipped off the light and walked out, leaving the bedroom door wide open.

"Come on. Let's go wake Kenny. They couldn't have gotten far."

The Brady brothers dressed in their stolen police uniforms and headed out the door with McKenzie.

Chapter 24

A Difficult Journey

The night was black, so Jesse switched on the flashlight the moment they stepped off the porch.

Skip looked up at the sky. The stars popped into view, but he couldn't find the moon. And being way out in the country, there were no city lights to illuminate their surroundings.

Thank God for that flashlight.

Skip and Jesse hiked a good distance from the house before they paused long enough to slip Suzi's shoes and socks on her feet. The shoes would keep her feet warm, and it was one less thing that Skip had to carry. The boys walked for almost two hours, seeing few houses along the long, lonely stretch of deserted road. Suzi slept soundly in her brother's arms the entire time.

Reaching an area with dense forest to their left, Skip paused. "Jesse, are we going the right way?"

Jesse looked up and down the road. "I haven't any idea. One thing I know for certain. I've never been here before."

"Me, neither. It would help tremendously if I hadn't made that long drive blindfolded. Cause I have a strange feeling that we're going the wrong way."

Jesse nodded. Reaching up, he lifted Suzi out of Skip's weary arms. "Let me carry her for awhile. She must be getting awfully heavy."

"She is." The moment his arms were empty, Skip felt his partner's cheeks and forehead. "You're feverish. You won't have to carry her long. I just need a little break."

While they hiked along the shoulder of the deserted road, a car approached in the distance. Skip waved his arms, beckoning for the driver to stop. The car slowed, but when the headlights illuminated their orange jumpsuits, the driver accelerated around them and took off. Skip sighed. A few minutes later another car came along, and the same thing happened.

"Can we rest a bit?" asked Jesse. "I'm so tired."

"Sure." Skip reached for his little sister, and Jesse passed the child to him. "Let's go into the woods where it's safer."

Skip led the way. It was so dark and secluded that they felt secure in settling down for a short rest. Yet, Skip didn't want to wander too far from the road for fear they'd get lost.

"Here's a good place." Hardly able to keep his eyes open, Skip sat down under a huge shade tree, leaning against it. Extending his legs out in front of him, he set his sister on one leg. Suzi rested her head against his chest and went back to sleep.

Jesse dropped down beside his partner and handed him the flashlight and the blanket. "Here, Skip. You use it for awhile."

Skip took the flashlight but refused the blanket. "I'm all right. I'll share Suzi's. Now why don't you lie down and get some sleep."

Without arguing, Jesse tossed the blanket on the ground. He curled up on it and wrapped it around himself, resting his head on Skip's other leg.

Embracing Suzi, with the blanket draped over them, helped warm Skip and his little sister. With a yawn, Skip rested his hand on Jesse's head. His partner was still feverish.

Skip leaned comfortably against the tree. "Lord, we're in a mess. Help us to evade our captors. Send Your angels to surround and protect us. Because we're wearing prison uniforms, come daybreak, everyone will be after us. They may shoot first and ask questions later. Touch Suzi and Jesse with Your healing power. Lord, I can't see what's going on around me, but I trust that even now You're looking after us."

A Score to Settle

Elated by the information that he and Kevin just uncovered, Johnny called Captain Kramer at 4:00 in the morning.

"Hello?"

"Captain, sorry about waking you, but..."

"You didn't wake me. I cannot sleep right now. Did you and Kevin find something?"

"Listen to this, Paul! The Brady brothers have a sister named Ariel. She lives in Converse County out in the country."

"Converse County! That's awfully big. Do you have an address?"

"Yes, it looks like she's south of Glenrock."

"Then run with it. We need to find Skip, Jesse, and Suzi before it's too late."

Johnny and Kevin had been on the case of their kidnapped comrades since noon yesterday, but they both worked days, and so far, they'd put in almost twenty-two hours. They were both running on fumes. Johnny was exhausted, but he wasn't about to let up until he'd found Skip and Jesse or collapsed in the attempt.

"Kevin, I'm running out to Converse County right now. I'll have a deputy meet me at this girl's house. Why don't you head home and get some sleep."

"I wouldn't sleep. Make the call. I'm going with you."

After phoning the Converse County Sheriff's Department, Johnny and Kevin dashed from the police station and jumped into a patrol car, racing out of town.

Skip rubbed the sleep from his eyes and looked up at his little sister, who stood there shaking him. He squinted and shaded his eyes from the glare of the early-morning sunrise peeking through the trees. He needed his dark glasses and suspected that they were still in the back seat of the Bradys' car.

"Skip, wake up."

"Hmm?" Skip blinked and looked up at her. Cupping her face in his hands, he felt for fever. "How do you feel, sweetheart?"

"Some better, but I'm so hungry."

"You're still running a mild fever." Skip glanced at his wristwatch. "Oh, my. I slept longer than I should have."

"Let's eat breakfast."

"Sweetheart, there is no breakfast."

"Then, let's go buy some."

"Oh, darling, that's a lot harder to do than it sounds."

"We can't go buy anything?" Suzi puckered.

Pulling her into his arms, Skip comforted her. "Afraid not, sweetie."

The child snuggled up to him and rested her head on his shoulder, starting to cry. "Skip, I'm so hungry my stomach hurts."

Tears burned his eyes as he embraced her tightly. "I'm so sorry, Suzi. Let's pray for some breakfast."

Suzi lifted her head and smiled at him. "Yeah. Jesus will take care of us."

"Yes, He will." Bowing their heads, Skip prayed, asking God to protect them from all danger, to help Jesse feel better, to get them home safely, and to provide breakfast for Suzi.

Skip kissed his little sister before setting her beside him. Then he gently nudged his sleeping partner. "Jesse, wake up. We need to get going."

Jesse slowly sat up. His face was flush. His eyes were glassy. And when Skip shook him, he felt the intense heat through Jesse's shirt. His partner was burning up with fever, and they had no water.

With a heavy sigh, Skip stood, brushed off his jumpsuit, shook out the blankets, and folded them for easy carrying. "Come on, Jesse." Skip lifted him to his feet. "I know you don't feel well, but we'll never get home if we stay here."

Jesse staggered, and Skip grasped his arm to steady him. Carrying the blankets, and holding onto Jesse's arm, Skip assisted him through the rough terrain back to the road. Suzi trailed them. Reaching the highway, he released Jesse's arm and looked both ways, at a loss to know which way was home. Skip turned east, which was the direction they originally headed when they escaped Ariel's house. If nothing else, they weren't returning to the place of their captivity.

"Skip, I'm tired of walking," said Suzi.

"All ready?" Skip knelt down and let her climb onto his back piggyback style.

Even with his young sister on his back, Skip attempted to flag down every passing motorist, but no one would stop. Between Suzi and the blankets, he was wearing down fast. And Jesse struggled to keep up with him.

"Look, Skip. A place to eat." Suzi squirmed in excitement and pointed straight ahead.

Skip paused, glancing hopefully at his partner. "I'll bet they have a phone. You think they'll let us use it?"

"Not when they see how we're dressed."

That deflated him, yet he knew Jesse was right. Their only chance might be to send Suzi in alone. *She was five-years-old. He would not send her into an unfamiliar establishment alone, especially not to protect him and Jesse.*

Collecting his courage, Skip hiked up to the door of the small café, and Jesse opened it for him. He didn't want to venture in too far, because he did not believe they'd receive a warm welcome. Still carrying his sister piggyback, Skip stepped into the restaurant, and Jesse followed him through the door.

A middle-aged man leaning on the counter drew back at the sight of two prison uniforms, and before Skip had a chance to say anything, he pulled a gun out from under the counter. "Get out!"

The boys scrambled out the door and around the side of the building to get out of the line of fire. Jesse grabbed Skip's arm to steady himself.

"You all right, partner?"

"I need some rest."

"I know, but we've got to keep going. Hold on to my arm."

Jesse leaned against Skip, clinging to his arm as they walked. They'd barely walked a quarter of a mile when

Skip spotted a house. Plodding up the front walk, he said a silent prayer.

Please, help us, Lord. Jesse needs something to drink. Suzi needs something to eat, and I need to use the telephone.

Unable to get a hand free to knock, Skip tapped the bottom of the door with his boot. A moment later, the door swung open. At the sight of them, the elderly woman turned deathly pale. Her look of fright and shock was followed by a slamming door. Skip cringed when he heard the dead bolt secure it tightly.

Skip sighed. "Jesse, these clothes are a curse."

"Skip, I'm hungry," said Suzi.

"I know you are. I am, too."

"Just a few minutes," said Jesse. "I'm so tired. Let's sit down for just a few minutes."

"All right, Jesse. Come on. I'll find a safe place for you to rest."

Crossing the street, Skip led them back into the forest. They hiked a distance from the main road before he felt it was safe to stop. Skip eased his sister to the ground and grasped Jesse's arm, helping him sit. Shaking out the blankets, he spread them on the ground for his partner to lay on. Suzi crawled up beside Jesse and lay down. Skip settled on the ground near them and leaned against a big tree. The day had warmed to the high 70's, but Jesse shivered.

"Come here, Suzi." Skip lifted her onto his lap and wrapped the blankets around his partner.

Suzi rubbed her eyes. "I want to lie down, too."

"You can lie down on me."

Straddling Skip, Suzi rested her head against his chest and relaxed in his arms. Skip closed his eyes. He didn't know how much longer he could carry the responsibility of a sick partner and little sister. Suzi exhausted him by constantly needing to be carried, and Jesse required a lot of support right now.

No one would help them. Everyone they'd come in contact with were scared off by the sight of prison uniforms. Many of those people had likely heard the news report warning them to be on the lookout for escaped convicts in the area, and advising them to notify authorities immediately because these desperate men were armed and dangerous.

And what about the real convicts? By now, the Brady brothers had discovered they'd taken off and were, no doubt, out looking for them. And while he and Jesse were dressed like convicts, Bryan and Kenny were probably impersonating cops.

But his greatest concern was the police, who could easily mistake them for the dangerous Brady brothers. They might be quick to shoot, and then they'd all be in trouble, because the cops would shoot to kill.

Chapter 25

The Search Continues

Johnny and Kevin met a county deputy at Ariel's house around sunrise.

The three officers approached the front door, and Deputy C.J. Graham rapped sharply. "I stopped by here right after you called, but there was no answer."

"Well, we have to try again." Johnny hammered the door with his fist.

"Things look mighty quiet," said Kevin. "This girl is going to hate us for getting her out of bed so early."

Johnny pounded on the door again. "She might. But that's a hazard that comes with the job."

C.J. threw up his hand for silence. "Do you guys hear that?"

"Help!" A faint voice came from inside the house. "Help! I'm trapped! Help!"

Yanking out their guns, the officers prepared to enter the house. C.J. tried the doorknob but found it locked. Johnny and Kevin flattened themselves against the wall on either side of the door, and C.J. kicked it in. Their guns ready, the officers stormed the house.

"Help!" The cry for help drifted down from the upstairs. "Let me out of here."

Separating, the three officers did a broad sweep of the huge house, searching for armed occupants before they finally followed the sound of the girl's voice to the bedroom at the top of the stairs. With their guns drawn, Johnny and Kevin followed Deputy Graham into the room.

"What took you so long?"

Johnny and Kevin exchanged glances with C.J., and they re-holstered their guns.

"And here we were worried about coming too early," said Kevin. "Who locked you in there?"

"My brother, Bryan. He and Kenny kidnapped two police officers and a little girl, but I helped them escape. So Bryan threw me in here. Then my brothers went after them. And there was another guy with them. A *big* guy."

Johnny caught his breath. *McKenzie!* He always seemed to be one step ahead of the police. "Which way did they go?"

"I don't know, but Skip and Jesse are wearing prison uniforms. They're in real danger."

Keying his mic, C.J. alerted the sheriff's department to Skip's and Jesse's plight.

"Stand back, Miss Brady." Johnny withdrew his gun.

Ariel retreated to the far side of the cage, her hands over her ears, and Johnny shot the lock off the door.

"Thank you." The girl stepped from her prison. "I don't know how I can ever repay you."

"Don't get mad about your front door," said C.J. "It'll probably need replaced."

"It's not safe for you to stay here," said Kevin. "Come with us. We'll put you into protective custody until your brothers have been recaptured.

"Let me pack a few things." Ariel dashed from the room.

Johnny turned to Kevin. "Are you okay to drive?"

"Yeah. It's amazing how adrenaline affects you. I'll probably collapse when I get home, though."

"Okay. Take Miss Brady with you to Forest Valley and arrange a safe-house for her. Her brothers won't find her there. Then go home and get some sleep. I'm going with Deputy Graham."

Suitcase in hand, Ariel followed Kevin outside to the Forest Valley cruiser.

Johnny climbed in with C.J., and they took off in search of Skip, Jesse, and Suzi.

Jason's stomach growled. Riding around in a police car looking for a couple of prison uniforms was boring, so he played around with the police radio until he located the channel used by the local sheriff's department. That way he could monitor radio traffic while he drove around.

And he put quite a few miles on the car. They'd been searching for those two cops for hours. How could they have disappeared so fast? They were on foot. Surely, no one gave them a ride, not a couple of men wearing prison uniforms.

With their vehicles parked on the shoulder of the highway, Jason unfolded a map and laid it on the warm hood of the police cruiser. Gathering around it, he and the Brady brothers studied it.

"They couldn't have gone far on foot," said Kenny.

Jason's finger traced a road on the map. "Okay, you guys were here. This is the road leading back to Forest Valley, and we know they're heading home."

"We've been up and down this road a dozen times," said Bryan. "They're on foot. There's no place for them to hide along here."

"There is up here." Jason slid his finger along the line on the map where it curved.

"Yeah, but look how far that is," said Kenny. "That's a good forty-minute drive from here. They're walking, carrying a sick child. There's no way they got that far. I'll bet you they went the other way."

Bryan glared at his brother. "Their homes are this way. Why in the world would they go the other way?"

Kenny raised an eyebrow like it was obvious. "And how would they know that? Neither of them knows which way we took them. One of them rode in the trunk and the other one was blindfolded."

Silence settled over the three men as they considered how logical that sounded. Just then, a broadcast on the police radio caught their attention, and Jason reached through the open cruiser window to turn it up.

"All units, be on the lookout for two escaped convicts matching the general description of Bryan and Kenneth Brady. These men are known to be armed and dangerous, so exercise extreme caution. They were last seen in the vicinity of Sherry Woods and may have a young child with them."

Jason grinned. "If that don't beat all. The police just solved our problem and told us where to find them."

"They did go the wrong way," said Kenny. "No wonder we couldn't find them."

"Okay, wait a minute." Bryan returned to the map. "We grew up playing in those woods." He tapped the location on the map. "We need to get in, grab that child and cop, and get out. Jason, whichever one you don't kill is the one we'll trade for Roy's release."

"Him and the kid," said Kenny.

Bryan nodded. "Yeah, we definitely want to hang onto that kid. They'll do anything to save a kid." Bryan traced the wooded area with his finger. "Apparently, they left the house and went the wrong way. If we circle around Sherry Woods this way and approach them from behind, we'll be able to grab them and avoid the police at the same time. But if they should spot us, all they'll see from a distance are police uniforms, and we'll blend right in with them." Bryan looked at Jason. "Then when you shoot yours, the police will think that one of their own shot him."

"Great plan," said Jason. "Let's go."

Scrambling into their vehicles, the three escaped prisoners took off. Bryan Brady led the way to Sherry Woods as he completed a u-turn, heading back the way they'd come and veering left down a side street which would take them to the backside of the woods.

Taking Fire

"Oh, my gosh! Did you hear that broadcast?" said Johnny. "They're going after Skip and Jesse."

C.J. whipped the cruiser around in the middle of the intersection. He flipped on his lights and sirens as they raced to Sherry Woods. Keying his mike, he reiterated his earlier broadcast, informing dispatch that the two men spotted in the area wearing prison uniforms were the two missing Forest Valley police officers.

With several reported sightings of two escaped convicts, and the Brady brothers still at large, the sheriff's department sent every available unit to search the woods and surrounding area. Already, the wooded area was crawling with police officers on the hunt for the two dangerous convicts. If necessary, officers were instructed to shoot to kill.

Deputy Robert Duncan crept through the brush with both hands on his gun, which he kept aimed at the ground. A splash of color caught his attention and he swung his gun that direction. Quickly lowering his aim, he inched toward the pink and yellow that flashed through the foliage.

There were the two escaped convicts he sought. If he radioed for backup, they'd likely hear him and bolt. He'd hold off sending a radio broadcast until he held them at gunpoint. Then they wouldn't escape.

Don walked softly. *Just a little closer,* he thought. A twig crunched under his boot, and he froze when one of the convicts looked around. He was only about twenty feet away when he aimed at one of the Brady brothers.

"Jesse, get up. I heard something."

Jesse? Don studied them closely. He was after Bryan and Kenny Brady. Had he inadvertently stumbled upon another set of escaped convicts? Escaped convicts that he'd heard nothing about? What were the chances of that happening?

Jesse struggled to his feet. Keeping the other guy in his sites, Don followed him with his gun. The man scrambled up with a little girl in his arms. Seeing the young child, he dropped his aim just as a gunshot exploded through the forest.

"Skip, they're shooting at us!" cried Jesse.

Skip? Don's mind raced. *Where had he recently heard those names before? Skip and Jesse.*

Snatching up the blankets and a flashlight, Skip bolted with the child in his arms, but Jesse tripped and fell.

"Come on, Jesse. We've got to get out of here!" Racing back to his friend, Skip dropped the flashlight and clasped Jesse's arm, pulling him to his feet.

Don caught his breath. He remembered where he'd heard those two names. *In briefing.* Skip and Jesse were the Forest Valley police officers who'd been abducted. Thank goodness he didn't shoot.

Several more gunshots exploded through the area.

But someone *was* shooting at them. Don scrutinized the area, looking for the gunman.

Skip and Jesse ran for cover while the child screamed.

"Hold your fire!" The command echoed through Don's radio. Two more shots rang out. "That's an order."

"Sarge, we're not shooting," radioed another officer. "We heard the radio broadcast."

"Then who's firing on them?"

Don keyed his mike. "The same people who are shooting at us."

Listening to the police radio, Johnny's heart raced. Skip, Suzi, and Jesse were in incredible danger, and he couldn't get there fast enough. C.J.'s cruiser skidded to a stop near a dozen other squad cars. He threw it into park. Johnny jumped from the car and dashed into the woods. C.J. raced after him, but gunfire made them dive for cover. The lieutenant scurried around to them.

Johnny scrutinized the wooded area before turning to the lieutenant. "Where are they? Where are Suzi, Skip, and Jesse? And who's shooting at them?"

"Calm down, Lieutenant Marshall."

"They're shooting at my kid brother, and all you can say is 'calm down.' Would you be calm if someone were shooting at your brother? Now, where are they?"

The lieutenant threw up his hands in surrender. "I don't know."

Johnny drew in a sharp breath, ready to unload on him for incompetence, but when he raised his right index finger, Johnny bit his tongue in silence.

The lieutenant said, "Moments before the first gunshot, C.J. radioed in with the vital information on the plight of your officers. I ordered my men to hold their fire and was promptly informed that they weren't the ones shooting.

"We believe that our escaped convicts are also in the area, and they're after these boys. At the sound of the first gunshot, your officers grabbed that child and bolted. We don't know where they went, and to be honest, at this point, they're not our priority. We want those convicts. And we are in the process of tracking them, aware that we have to catch them before they catch up with your men."

Chapter 27

An Avenue of Escape

Ducking behind heavy brush, Skip tightly embraced his little sister. Sobbing, Suzi screamed and clung to him.

"Shh, Suzi, you've got to be real quiet. You mustn't cry."

Suzi buried her face in his jumpsuit, trembling uncontrollably, yet stifling her sobs. For a moment, all gunfire ceased, but the brief silence was broken by the sound of a helicopter. Skip and Jesse looked up.

"That's a police chopper," said Skip. "They're looking for us."

"But why are they shooting at us? We're not armed."

More gunshots rang out.

"They don't know that. We've got to get out of here." With the blankets draped over his left arm and supporting the weight of his young sister, Skip whispered in her ear. "Hold on tight."

Suzi wrapped both arms around his neck and laid her head on his shoulder.

Grasping Jesse's left arm, Skip pulled him to his feet, and they ran. Jesse stumbled and staggered, but Skip's strong grip kept him moving without falling. While they ran, Skip prayed.

Lord, send a couple of angels to shelter us. We need help, and we need it now!

Reaching the highway, Skip dragged Jesse into the middle of the street. An approaching car skidded and swerved to avoid running over them. Having brought the vehicle to a complete stop, Skip released Jesse and yanked open the back door.

The two college-age girls in the front seat stared at him in horror when he shoved Jesse into their car and scrambled into the back seat beside him with Suzi in his arms. He slammed the door shut.

"Drive! Get us out of here."

Trembling at the thought of a gun pointed at her, Teri Carson accelerated back into her own lane. *I never forget to lock the back door. How could I make such a mistake, especially with escaped convicts in the area?*

A police helicopter circled overhead, but to Teri's dismay, it didn't follow them. That meant the police didn't know those convicts had jumped into her car.

Passing several state and county police vehicles parked on the shoulder of the road, the girls exchanged terrified looks.

Karen and I are as good as dead. Collecting every ounce of courage, Teri spoke, attempting to hide the tremor in her voice. "Please don't hurt us."

"We're not going to hurt you. We're police officers, not convicts."

"Then why are you wearing prison uniforms?" asked Karen.

"This may be hard for you to believe, but we were abducted and forced to put them on at gunpoint."

Teri frequently glanced at the lad's reflection through her rear view mirror. He looked almost as frightened as she felt. Yet, his voice was calm and gentle. She expected an escaped convict running from the police to be harsh and abrasive.

"And the mere sight of these clothes sends people after us with guns. Even now, the police are out there looking for us, while the real convicts have our police uniforms."

"That does sound a little unbelievable," said Karen.

"Unfortunately for us, you're right. My name is Skip. This is my partner, Jesse, and my little sister, Suzi."

"I'm Karen, and this is my roommate, Teri."

Regardless of their exceptional circumstances, Teri noticed how her comrade relaxed tremendously after talking to Skip. Shifting positions, she glanced into the rear view mirror at the faces of her other two passengers. Skip's partner, Jesse, had leaned his head back against the seat and closed his eyes. His face was bruised and flushed. He'd obviously taken a beating, and he looked sick. But Skip's little sister was no more than five or six years old. Teri's eyes widened at the sight of her.

Obviously bone-weary, they all three looked familiar. Where had she seen them before? Frequently glancing into her rear view mirror, her eyes bounced from one passenger to the next. The child snuggled up to her handsome brother. He embraced her tenderly while gazing absently out the window. And these two were supposed to be desperate convicts trying to escape? Neither of them even watched her and Karen.

The news! That's where she'd seen their faces, yet uncertainty clouded her memory. If she could get a good look at Skip, she'd recognize him.

"Skip?"

"Miss?" The boy turned and looked directly at her.

Teri grinned. He called her 'miss.' These guys were, indeed, the missing Forest Valley police officers. "Where would you like to go?"

"We live in Forest Valley, but we'd be delighted if you even dropped us off at the nearest police station," said Skip.

"What do you think, Karen?"

"Oh, let's live on the edge and take them all the way to Forest Valley."

Skip brushed the back of his hand against Jesse's forehead. "You're burning up. How do you feel?"

"Miserable."

Sitting on Skip's lap, Suzi started to cry and rested her head against his chest. "I'm hungry and thirsty. Please, Skip, let's eat."

Cuddling his little sister, Skip breathed a sigh and blinked back the tears that burned his eyes. He had no money on him. The Brady brothers had taken his wallet.

Karen patted the seat beside her. "Come sit up front with us, Suzi. That way Jesse can lie down. He's not feeling well."

Suzi looked at Skip for approval. With a grin, Skip nodded. Suzi climbed into the front seat, and Karen secured the middle seat belt around her.

Jesse curled up on the back seat and went to sleep, his head in Skip's lap. Yet, despite his high fever, he shivered, so Skip covered him with a blanket. Fanning himself, he lowered his window. A few minutes into their ride, Teri pulled into the drive-through of a fast-food restaurant.

"Here we are, Suzi-Q. What do you want to eat?"

"Do they have chicken nuggets?"

"You bet. Skip, what would you like?"

"Thank you, Teri, but I'm fine."

"You're starving! I can hear your stomach growling all the way up here. How about a double decker cheeseburger, fries, and a medium cola?"

Skip grinned. "Thank you. I'd like that."

"Would Jesse like something to eat?" asked Teri.

"He's asleep."

"Okay." Teri turned to the window and ordered lunch for them all. As she drove from the parking lot, Karen distributed the food. "Here, Skip, this is for Jesse." She handed him two aspirin tablets and a cup of water. "Wake him up to take this aspirin."

"Yes, miss."

Skip shook his partner and helped him sit up, dropping the aspirin tablets into his hand. Jesse popped them into his mouth and emptied the cup of water. Then he lay back down.

Suzi wasted no time devouring her chicken nuggets and fries, washing them down with a carton of milk. Curling up on the front seat, she laid her head in Karen's lap and fell asleep. Skip wolfed down his cheeseburger and fries before emptying his cup of soda. His stomach now full, he rested his head against the cloth seat and closed his eyes, drifting into a light sleep. A sudden shout startled him awake.

"A road block!"

Shifting in his seat, he peeked out the windshield. "That's strange. Why would they set up a road block with a privately owned vehicle?" His eyes zeroed in on the three men wearing police uniforms and tennis shoes. "Those men are escaped convicts, Teri. Don't stop! Don't stop!"

"They're in uniforms."

"Yeah, mine and Jesse's. They're not cops!"

Sliding out from under Jesse, Skip dropped to the floor behind the passenger's seat. He covered Jesse completely with the blanket, then pulled it over himself.

Jason paced anxiously in front of Morgan's patrol car. He couldn't believe they escaped detection with the area crawling with cops and a police chopper circling overhead.

Bryan and Kenny leaned comfortably against their sister's red Taurus with their hands in their pockets and their legs crossed at the ankles. How could his buddies stand there looking so nonchalant? For all they knew, the police had already figured out that they weren't cops, and the cops were closing in on them from every direction.

He jumped when a green sedan came into view, gradually slowing to a stop long before it reached them.

"Oh, it's just a couple of college kids," said Bryan. "You take this one, Jason. You have a couple of daughters the ages of those girls."

The sedan crawled to a stop just a few feet short of their roadblock. Approaching the driver's side, Jason glanced back at his pals. "Thanks a lot."

Kenny grinned. "Hey, it was your idea to set up a roadblock. You're the one after a specific cop. To us, any cop will do."

The driver lowered her window and smiled nervously at Jason.

"Good morning, ladies," said Jason. "Just a routine traffic stop. What's under the blankets?" He reached through the open rear window.

"Oh, I wouldn't, officer. That's our pet bull dog, Bruno," said the dark-haired driver.

Jason froze.

The passenger nodded her pretty head in agreement. "He's sleeping right now, and we don't want to do anything that would wake him up with you here." Reaching behind her, she gently patted the blanket. The pit bull shifted positions, and Jason yanked his arm back so fast, the girls burst into laughter.

"Why?"

"Because he really hates cops. You should see what he did to the last police officer."

"Teri! Hush."

"Well, I've got to warn him. That poor officer. After the incident, he had to retire from the force. His arm was so mangled that he could no longer hold a gun. Officer, may we go? We're late for a party."

"Of course. Drive safely and have a nice day. Jason slid behind the wheel of the patrol car and backed it up to allow them through.

Stepping from the cruiser, he looked at the Brady brothers. "I wonder what kind of party they were attending. I wouldn't take a child that small to a party."

Bryan bolted upright. "Child? What child?"

"The little girl in the front seat. If you had approached the car with me, you would have seen her."

"Describe her," said Bryan. "What was she wearing?"

Jason shrugged. "Typical kid. About five or six, blonde hair, wearing a yellow shirt and pink jumper."

"Th-th-that girl was the child with those two cops! You've been had by a couple of college kids," said Bryan.

"Now, how was I supposed to know that?" Jason jumped into the police cruiser and took off in pursuit. Kenny and Bryan scrambled into their car and followed him.

Chapter 28

Joining the Chase

Johnny couldn't get his mind off Skip and the danger he was in. He would cry if anything happened to Jesse or Suzi, but he wasn't certain he could go on if he lost his best friend.

The shooting had stopped, and he had one prevailing thought – to find his friends and get them out of there. He thoroughly scanned the area for any sign of his comrades. They were here somewhere, either in hiding or injured and unable to get to the police for help.

C.J. grabbed his arm. "Let's go."

"Go where? I'm not leaving without Skip, Jesse, and Suzi."

"Johnny, we have to find those escaped convicts before they kill someone with their random shooting."

"They weren't shooting randomly. They were shooting at Skip and Jesse."

"All the more reason to want them in custody."

"I'm not leaving, C.J. They're in these woods somewhere, maybe hurt or dying. I have to find them."

"They're cops, Johnny. They didn't wait around to be shot. They got out of the line of fire. It's my guess that they're in hiding right now, and no one will be able to find them. Now, we have to find those convicts. They are our priority. Once they're back in custody, we can return to look for your people. And we will. So are you coming with me or staying here?"

Johnny wrestled with the idea of leaving without thoroughly searching the area for Suzi and the boys, but then, he didn't know if they were still in the woods, and he was about to collapse from exhaustion. It made sense to stay with C.J. for now.

"I'm coming."

Following him to the police cruiser, Johnny slid in beside him, and they took off. On high alert, the state police and sheriff's department had joined forces as they actively combed the area for the escaped convicts, hoping to cross paths with the missing police officers during their intense search.

C.J. turned onto the highway toward Forest Valley, watching for anything that could lead him to those convicts.

Teri kept a watchful eye in the rear view mirror, fearful that those convicts detected something amiss in her story and would give chase. Within a minute of passing through their roadblock, their vehicles came into view.

"They're following us," she said.

Just then a bullet hit the bumper of the car.

Karen gasped. "And shooting at us! Step on it, Teri!"

Teri floored the accelerator, frequently glancing in her rear view mirror to see if they were gaining on her. That phony cop chased them in the Forest Valley police cruiser, while the red Taurus raced after him. A few minutes later, a state patrol car joined the chase. Then another police vehicle fell in line.

Skip started to crawl out from under the blanket.

"Stay down," said Karen.

Teri slammed on the brake to make a right-hand turn, and the car squealed around the corner. Awakened with a start, Suzi started to cry and sat up. Pulling the child into her arms, Karen comforted her.

"Shh, it's okay."

The Forest Valley police car followed her, but the red Taurus continued straight through the intersection without turning. Watching through her rear view mirror, Teri saw that most of the police cars followed the Taurus.

Constantly checking her rear view mirror, she saw a sheriff's car fall in line behind the Forest Valley cruiser. She suspected that before the day was over, she and

Karen would be calling their parents to come bail them out of jail, but they were in too deep to stop now.

Jesse sat up on the back seat and looked around. Skip sat down beside him, watching the activity through the rear window.

Without warning, the Forest Valley cruiser crossed the dotted yellow line and zipped passed her, disappearing around the bend up ahead. But the police officer who was still behind her turned on his flashing lights.

"Oh, no," groaned Teri. "Now that sheriff's deputy is pulling me over. We're in big trouble."

"Pull over, Teri. That's a real cop," said Skip.

Johnny wasn't certain what was going down. He was too tired to think clearly, so he was glad that C.J. was behind the wheel of the car.

"Weren't we in pursuit of a red Taurus?" he asked. "How come we turned?"

"You don't know what happened?"

"No. I think I might have dozed off."

C.J. laughed. "The Taurus is carrying two of our escaped convicts, likely Kenneth and Bryan Brady. The other police cars will follow them while we pull over the car they were chasing."

The green sedan pulled onto the shoulder of the road and C.J. coasted to a stop directly behind it.

Johnny stepped from the cruiser and lingered on the passenger's side of the sedan watching the hands of all the occupants and searching for a weapon. C.J. approached the driver's window. With a dark tint shading the back windows, Johnny could barely make out two male passengers in the backseat. All he cared about at this point was that neither of them pulled a gun.

The young female driver lowered her window.

"Hands where I can see them," said C.J.

Every adult in the car complied with his command, and Johnny saw hands go up all over the car.

C.J. looked into the backseat and grinned. Reaching for the back door, he pulled it open, motioning for the boys in the backseat to get out of the car.

Johnny anxiously watched as the two guys who climbed from the car had the word 'Inmate' stamped on the back of their orange jumpsuits. It took a minute to sink it.

"Skip!" Sprinting around the car, Johnny pulled Skip into his arms, embracing him tightly.

Skip wanted to melt into Johnny's arms. Johnny's brotherly embrace had never felt so good.

The deputy reached into the front seat and lifted Suzi into his arms. "I take it, you're Suzi. You come with us, sweetheart."

Releasing Skip, Johnny gave Jesse a quick hug. "Man, I thought I might never see you guys again."

"We were wondering about that ourselves," said Jesse.

"Well, you guys are in the clear," said Deputy Graham, still carrying Suzi. "Jump into the patrol car, and I'll run you home as soon as I talk to these young ladies."

"May I talk to them first?" Skip stepped up to Teri's window and grasped her hand. "Thanks for everything. If you'll give me your address, I'll send you a check to cover your expenses, like buying us lunch, using your gasoline, and donating your time, which was invaluable under the circumstances."

"Skip, this was an adventure I'll never forget. And it was well worth our time and money." Teri jotted down her address and folded the slip of paper into Skip's hand. "But I would love to keep in touch and know how you, Suzi, and Jesse are doing from time to time. Would you send me a picture?"

"I sure will. Thanks again, Teri." Skip squeezed her hand and released her.

Turning to the deputy, he lifted his sleepy little sister into his arms and carried her to the sheriff's car, where Jesse had already climbed into the back.

Johnny walked to the car with him, opening the back door for Skip before wearily sliding into the front passenger's seat. Seating Suzi in the middle, Skip slid in beside her, watching the deputy as he talked to Teri and Karen. He jotted notes while he talked to them. A few minutes later, he backed away from their sedan and waved. Teri completed a u-turn and honked as she drove back the way she'd come.

C.J. slid behind the wheel of his car and keyed his mic, briefing the lieutenant on his encounter with the occupants of the green sedan and requesting permission to run his car-load of passengers home, which was nearly a ninety minute drive away.

"When you get into Forest Valley, take them straight to the hospital. I'll notify the Forest Valley PD that you're en route with their three officers and the young child, and that you should arrive around noon."

"Yes, sir." Cranking the car engine, C.J. pulled onto the highway and accelerated up to speed. He glanced over at Johnny, who was sound asleep in the front seat.

C.J. smiled and turned up his police radio so he could listen to the verbal exchange on the recent pursuit. They just caught the Brady brothers. This was shaping up to be a positive day. No one was injured from all the shooting. They recovered the three kidnap victims, and they recaptured two of the escaped convicts.

With all his passengers asleep, it was a quiet ride into Forest Valley. C.J. still had to question Skip and Jesse before he could release them. Suzi, too. He'd talk to them when they reached the hospital.

Rose and her sons had finally arrived at the airport and checked in for their flight. She was fortunate enough to catch a direct flight into Fenton Regional Airport, the closest airport to Forest Valley. And their flight was scheduled to leave at noon. That should get them home about 2:30. And boy did she have a lot to tell Erin.

While Trevor and Robby explored the gift shops near their departure gate, Rose buried herself in a novel that she finally had the time to read. She was halfway through chapter six when Trevor interrupted her.

"Mom, did you hear the announcements? Our flight has been delayed."

"What? Why?" asked Rose.

"Something's not right with the plane," said Robby. "They're having some type of mechanical difficulties."

Rose sighed. "Do they have any idea how long we'll be delayed?"

"No. But they're hoping it's not too long," said Trevor. "I guess we'll just have to wait and see."

"While we're waiting, let's get lunch," said Robby. "I'm hungry."

Rose agreed. "Good idea. Let me call your Aunt Erin and tell her that our flight has been delayed. Rose found a phone and placed the call, but Erin's phone just rang. No one answered it.

C.J. finally pulled into town. He'd never been to Forest Valley before, so he had no idea which direction took him to the hospital. He'd have to stop and ask.

Glancing back at his sleeping passengers, he sighed. He really didn't want to wake anyone, but he needed directions. Where were the townspeople? The streets looked practically deserted. At least, there were no pedestrians out and about.

Sitting at a red light, he wondered if he should turn right, turn left, go straight, or wake Johnny. Just then, a police car cruised through the light at the intersection in front of him. C.J. rounded the corner behind him and flashed his headlights. The police unit in front of him made a u-turn and pulled up alongside him with his window lowered.

One glance into C.J.'s car, and the officer grinned. "Follow me."

C.J. trailed him to the hospital, hardly expecting what he saw when he turned into the circle drive at the emergency department entrance. There were dozens of people waiting for him, and when they saw him pull in, they started cheering. But the instant he stopped his car, chaos erupted.

Chapter 29

Ariel's Visit

Several people converged on his cruiser at once, yanking open the back doors. Sound asleep against the car door, Skip tumbled out of the car into the arms of another police officer.

C.J. shifted to park and cut the engine. Slowly stepping from his squad car, he watched the commotion. There had to be a half dozen uniformed police officers there. Skip was surrounded by people hugging and kissing him. After kissing Skip, a woman reached into the back seat of his car and lifted the five-year-old into her arms, embracing and kissing her.

She must be their mother, thought C.J.

A couple of officers helped Jesse out of the car and walked him around the car to the ED entrance where a young woman greeted him. She threw her arms around his neck and pulled him into a warm embrace. The police captain opened Johnny's car door to talk to him.

Softly closing his car door, C.J. stepped onto the walk, observing the outpouring of concern and love for the two missing officers and young child. As the Emergency Department technicians escorted them into the ED, and their families followed, the supportive crowd started to scatter. Johnny left with another uniformed officer.

C.J. followed Skip and Jesse into the hospital. He hated the thought of disrupting this glorious family reunion, but he had a lot of questions that needed answered in order to write a complete report.

While waiting to be examined by the doctor, Skip talked to Deputy Graham. Captain Kramer remained with his officers throughout the deputy's questioning and the doctor's examination.

Cassandra never left Skip's side, while his mother stayed with Suzi. When it was finally his turn to be examined, he learned that Suzi and Jesse had been admitted to the hospital, so when the doctor ordered him admitted for observation, it didn't surprise him.

Skip didn't want to stay, but he was so exhausted, he didn't have the energy to refuse, not that Captain Kramer would have allowed it. He and Jesse were roommates, and their captain stayed with them until they were settled into their room, talking to them before he left.

Cassandra and Jackie weren't allowed to stay with them because the doctor wanted them to get some rest. So once they were through the emergency department system, their wives left the hospital, promising to return later.

Skip slept all afternoon. Opening his eyes, he gazed across the room at his partner. "Jesse?"

Jesse's wife, Jackie, sat beside his bed holding his hand.

Cassandra rubbed Skip's arm. "He's still asleep. How do you feel?"

Skip sat up in bed and looked at her. "I'm hungry. How long have you ladies been here?"

"About a half hour."

"Where's Mom?"

"She's with Suzi."

"Where is Suzi?"

"She's on the third floor in the children's wing. Since you and Suzi showed no signs of physical abuse, you'll be released as soon as you talk to a counselor. But they want to keep Jesse overnight."

Skip looked at his sleeping partner, and caught sight of the tears trickling down Jackie's cheeks. "Jackie?" Sliding off the bed wearing a hospital gown, he started toward her.

"Oh, Skip." Jackie exploded into tears and ran into his arms.

"Shh, it's okay. Jesse will be all right." Skip held her, letting her cry.

There was a soft knock at the door, and Ariel poked her head in. "Hi. Mind if I come in?"

"Not at all," said Skip.

Kevin followed her into the room.

"Now that my brothers are back in prison, it's safe for me to return home. But I wanted to stop and see how you fellows are doing." Stepping over to Jesse's bed, she rested her hand on his forehead. "He's not too hot. I think he's over the worst of it."

"Ariel, this is Jesse's wife, Jackie," said Skip. "And my wife, Cassandra."

"I'm pleased to meet you." Ariel graciously offered each one her hand before turning to Skip. She enveloped his right hand between both of hers. "Thank you. I know you didn't have a choice, but I was a prisoner in my own home until they brought you home. You and Jesse are very brave."

"So are you." Skip squeezed her hand. "Thank you for everything you did for us."

Ariel smiled. "Bye, Skip. Maybe you could bring Suzi to see me some time." She kissed him on the cheek and stepped over to Jesse's bed, kissing him also. "Bye, Jesse."

"Bye, Ariel." Jesse spoke barely above a whisper.

"Skip, where's Suzi? I want to kiss her good-bye, too"

"She's in room 302," said Cassandra.

"Thanks." With a contented sigh, Ariel left.

Kevin called after her. "I'll meet you down in the lobby."

"Okay."

"Skip?" chimed Cassandra and Jackie.

"It's, uh..." Skip looked at Kevin. "It's not what you think. Really."

"It's not, huh?" said Cassandra. "What do we think?"

"Um..."

Jackie and Cassandra giggled at him, entertained by his embarrassment. Kevin crossed his arms and studied Skip with amusement.

"Ariel's a nice girl."

"Yeah, we could see that," said Jackie. "Friendly, too."

"And she was kind to us."

Cassandra nodded in agreement. "Now, that was obvious."

Kevin started laughing.

"No, no. N-n-not like that. She helped us escape."

"How sweet of her," said Jackie.

"Jesse, will you help me out here?"

"No need. You're digging a hole deep enough for both of us."

The girls burst into laughter. "You're cute, Skip," said Jackie. "I can't get Jesse flustered like that."

"Well, I got to run Ariel home," said Kevin. "The captain told me to stop by the PD and pick up your uniforms, wallets, guns, and gun belts while I was out that way. And for the record, Ariel is a nice girl." He winked at Skip and trotted out the door.

Jason parked the stolen cruiser behind the motel where he was hiding out. He slammed the car door and stormed into the room, kicking the door shut. Brent glanced up at him, bleary eyed from lack of sleep.

"Oh, I forgot about you." Jason kicked off his shoes and removed the gun belt he wore. "That kid got away again. He's slick as baby oil."

With tape over his mouth, Brent made muffled noises, but Jason ignored him. Stripping off the police uniform, he sprawled onto the bed for a quick nap.

After a brief snooze, Jason once again pulled on the police uniform and grabbed the telephone, slamming it down beside Morgan before yanking the tape off his mouth. Brent's glassy, blood shot eyes filled with terror when Jason held a gun to his head.

"I don't need you. But I'm tired of playing cat and mouse with Shaughnessy. I want his address! Get it for me, or I'll shoot you within the hour."

Chapter 30

Forced to Fight

Skip showered and changed into the fresh clothes that Cassandra brought him. After discussing their ordeal with a counselor, he and Suzi were released from the hospital.

Suzi thoroughly enjoyed the wheelchair ride down the corridor, while Skip would have preferred to walk, but it was hospital policy. When they reached the hospital entrance, his mother's van sat parked at the curb in the circle drive between two police cars.

The nurses wheeled Skip and Suzi out to her vehicle. Slowly standing, Skip glanced from one police cruiser to the other. Opening the back door, he buckled in his little sister before sliding into the front beside his mother.

"Mom, is it really necessary we have a police escort home?"

"It wasn't my idea. Chief Clark sent them."

"Oh." This was not good. If the chief sent two officers to escort him home from the hospital, then he was in grave danger. McKenzie was still out there. That man would be the death of him yet.

It was a good half-hour drive from the hospital to his house. All the way home, they followed Officer Greg Foster, while Officer Tim DeShea followed them. If Greg drove through a yellow light, his mother and Tim followed him through on red. Nothing separated their three-car caravan.

Finally reaching his house, Greg pulled up to the curb, and Tim coasted into the driveway right behind them. Suzi leaped from the car and raced into the house. Greg waved and drove away, but Tim trailed Skip and his mother toward the house, detaining them on the front porch.

"Mrs. Shaughnessy, until Jason McKenzie is back in custody, your house will be closely monitored by the police. I'm sorry we can't offer you round the clock protection, but our manpower is sadly lacking. If anything happens, call us immediately. We can have a unit here in two minutes. I would recommend everyone stay in the house at all times. I wouldn't even send the girls to school right now."

Erin nodded her assent and quietly entered the house.

Tim turned to Skip. "That means you, too, Shaun. You have to stay home, inside the house, if for no other reason than to help protect your family. And those orders are from Chief Clark."

"He doesn't even want me at work?"

"No. You are not to leave this house until McKenzie is back in custody. Is that clear?"

"Yes, sir."

Rose stood at a payphone, listening to Erin's phone ring and ring and ring. No one picked up.

Where is everyone, she thought. *It's Saturday evening. Surely, someone's home.* She just wanted to tell them that they would be home closer to 10:00. When they couldn't get the plane fixed in a timely manner, they changed planes. And their flight was about to leave.

"Mom, we gotta go," said Robby. "Or we'll miss our flight."

Rose sighed and hung up the phone. "All right."

Robby grabbed her carry-on and led them through the breezeway where a stewardess stood waiting for them.

"Thank you so much for waiting for us," said Rose.

Hands in his pockets, Skip stood on the front step, watching his fellow officer slide into the patrol car and drive away. Stepping into the house, he quietly closed and bolted the front door.

Suzi was the center of attention.

"Suzi, are you okay?" Sandy embraced and kissed her little sister.

Suzi nodded. "Thanks to Skip. He's brave."

Spotting Skip, four-year-old Scooter raced to him, leaping into his arms. "'Kip!"

Skip scooped her up and kissed her cheek. "How's my little Scooter Pie?"

Sandy and Stephanie ran to their brother, throwing their arms around him. Suzi sighed when her sisters' affection and attention suddenly turned to Skip.

"Skip, what happened?" said Stephanie. "Where were you and Suzi? Why didn't you come home?"

"It's a long story, Stephie." Skip slid his arm around Sandy and gave her a quick hug. After setting Scooter down, he slid his hand under Stephanie's chin and kissed her rosy cheek. "Sweetie, I don't feel like talking about it right now, but I'll bet Suzi will tell you all about it."

In a flurry of sudden movement, Skip's little sisters abandoned him, racing back to Suzi.

"Suzi, tell us what happened," said Sandy.

Once again the center of attention, Suzi beamed and glanced at Skip. Skip winked at her. Sliding his hands into his pockets, he strolled into the kitchen where his mother was talking to their next door neighbor.

"They've been fed," said Ruth Miller. "And they are wired. They've had a hard time settling down, especially Scooter."

"That's to be expected under the circumstances."

"You may have difficulty getting them to bed."

Erin glanced toward the open kitchen door, listening to the excited chatter from the other room. Her face glowed at the sight of her son. "Last night they were crying. I much prefer seeing them bubble over with excitement. Ruth, how can I ever thank you for watching them on such short notice?"

Ruth laughed and winked at Skip. "Erin, when haven't I watched them on short notice? For twenty years I've been known as the Shaughnessys' short-notice baby-sitter."

"You're exaggerating," said Erin.

"Am I? Well, I have to run. Todd and I are flying to West Virginia to visit our daughter and her family. And our plane leaves in a couple of hours."

"How long will you be away?" asked Skip.

"A week. Will you keep an eye on the house while we're gone?"

"Most certainly," said Erin.

"I gave Stephanie a house key so she could feed the fish every day while we're away," said Ruth.

"Have a nice trip, and we'll see you when you get back," said Erin.

Ruth slipped out the kitchen door, and Skip re-locked it.

"Well, I don't guess anybody's hungry but me," said Erin. "You and Suzi ate dinner at the hospital, and Ruth fed the girls."

Slipping into the kitchen, Cassandra embraced Skip from behind and kissed his smooth cheek. "It's good to have you safe at home. With you and Suzi missing last night, your mom and I didn't sleep very well."

"That's an understatement. We didn't sleep at all."

Cassandra smiled. "That may be true, but we did try."

Folding Cassandra into his arms, Skip cuddled her as he glanced at his watch. It was only 7:30.

"Are you trying to tell me that you're tired and want to go to bed?" asked Skip.

Snuggling up to him, Cassandra rested her head against his chest and closed her eyes. "How very perceptive of you. That's exactly what I'm trying to say."

With one arm around his young wife, Skip stroked her cheek and fingered her long auburn hair. Sliding his hand under her chin, he raised her head and kissed her. "Thanks for waiting up for me last night, Cassandra. I'll see you in the morning."

Cassandra kissed Skip and shuffled upstairs to bed.

"Son, did you want something to eat?" asked Erin.

"No, thanks, Mom. I'm not hungry."

Leaving the kitchen, Skip crept back into the living room and crouched low as he sneaked up on his young sisters. Seeing him crawl out from behind the recliner, the girls screamed and scattered, running in different directions. Suzi and Sandy scampered up the stairs while Stephanie grabbed Scooter and ran for the kitchen. Skip chased Sandy and Suzi up the stairs, but by the time he reached the top, the girls had already disappeared.

Quietly, Skip crept into his bedroom. His two young sisters screamed and threw pillows at him as they raced past him out the door.

Skip chased them down the stairs. "Don't scream!" he yelled. "Cassandra's sleeping."

Erin dashed from the kitchen. "Skip, what on earth are you doing, stirring them up like that?"

"Having fun, Mom."

"I can see that, but ..."

The four young girls ran in circles around their brother and started back up the stairs, sounding like a herd of buffalo. Skip started up the stairs after them and jerked to a sudden stop. Despite the racket they were making, he heard the back door slam against the wall. Leaping over the banister, Skip dropped to the floor, ducking behind the wall. How he wished he had a gun.

His police issue Glock was at the Converse County Sheriff's Department. His rifle was locked up in his gun case, and the key was probably still in his uniform trouser pocket.

Reaching the top of the stairs, Stephanie realized that Skip didn't follow them, so she started back down the stairs looking for him. She gasped when a strange man exploded onto the scene and grabbed her mother. With her brother still downstairs, she knew that he would protect their mother, but she had to safeguard the younger ones. Stephanie bolted up the stairs and corralled her sisters into their mother's bedroom.

"Hide in the closet. And don't come out until I tell you to."

Suzi giggled. "Skip will never find us in here."

The girls hid in the closet and closed the door.

Stephanie snatched up the phone to call the police. *Oh, no, the line is dead.*

A Score to Settle

Skip crouched low, fearing that his mother or one of his young sisters might get caught in the middle of all this. He needed the telephone, but it was mounted to the wall in the kitchen.

"Where's your son?" came an irritated male voice.

Wonderful. McKenzie had his mom cornered.

"I don't know." Erin's voice trembled.

"All right, kid, you show yourself, or your mother dies."

Skip slowly stood, his hands in the open. There stood Jason McKenzie at the bottom of the stairs wearing a police uniform and tennis shoes. With a firm grip on Erin's arm, he held her at gunpoint.

"You came for me, so let her go."

With a gleam in his eye, McKenzie released Erin and withdrew a set of handcuffs from the case on the police belt around his waist. He thrust them into her hand. "Cuff him. Behind his back."

Tears coursing down her cheeks, Erin snapped the handcuff bracelet on Skip's left wrist.

Taking her son's right wrist, Erin brought his arms behind his back and handcuffed him loosely. Skip silently studied McKenzie.

"Now, it's your turn, lady." Jerking her arms behind her back, McKenzie securely bound her wrists together. Then he shoved her into the living room. "Sit down! Up against the wall."

Sobbing, Erin did as she was told.

I can't believe this is happening, thought Skip. *Lord, if you don't do something, I'll soon be joining my father. Not that I would mind. I'll bet Heaven's lovely this time of year.* Skip grinned at the thought.

"You think it's funny, huh, kid?"

Skip sighed. "No, I was just thinking of my father."

"Your father's dead."

"Actually, he's more alive than you and I, Mr. McKenzie. Right now, he's in Heaven, living with Jesus."

McKenzie clenched Skip's shirt, forcing him into the middle of the living room. "I killed him, just like I'm going to kill you."

"Then I'll go to Heaven to live with Jesus."

"No!" cried Erin.

McKenzie shoved Skip. "You talk like a loony toon. You actually sound happy that I'm going to kill you."

"No, I'm not. I have a family to take care of." Skip nodded toward his crying mother. "If you kill me, they will suffer. I'd be in Heaven. How about you, Mr. McKenzie? Do you know Jesus as your Savior so when you die, you will go to Heaven?"

With his gun pointed at Skip, McKenzie's hands began to tremble. "Uh, l-l-let's change the subject. D-d-do you know a cop by the name of Brent Morgan?"

"Unfortunately, I do."

"Unfortunately is right. If it hadn't been for him, I never would have located you. He's a Forest Valley cop that doesn't deserve to live because of everything he did. He's nothin' but a traitor. So before you die, I will allow you the privilege of passing judgment on him. Name the sentence and after I shoot you, I will gladly execute it."

"How thoughtful. I suppose you know exactly where to locate him, too."

"Of course. I have him tied up back at my hideout. Believe me, Shaughnessy, he ain't going nowhere. Now, why don't you let me kill him for you?"

"Don't do me any favors," said Skip. "I'd like you to let him go."

"Let him go? After what he did to you? Why?"

"For several reasons. I forgive him. He's ignorant and didn't know what he was doing. Also, he has a wife and son who need him. But the biggest reason is that he's not ready to die. He'd go to hell, Mr. McKenzie. He doesn't know Jesus as his Savior, either."

Skip glanced at the gun. McKenzie's hands started trembling again.

"Shut up, Shaughnessy! You're starting to sound like my daughter. I don't want to hear any more." He slowly approached Skip, his finger on the trigger.

Skip studied his eyes. "Mr. McKenzie, you came to kill me. Please free Morgan, and spare my mother the anguish of witnessing the senseless death of her only son."

"No! I won't release Morgan. He deserves to die. And as for your mother, I'll spare her."

Erin gasped when McKenzie turned the gun on her. It looked like they would both be joining Stephen before the day was out. Her mind flew to her young daughters who had run upstairs, and she said a silent prayer that God would keep them in His loving care.

Spinning around, Skip cracked McKenzie's wrist with a crescent kick, followed by a back kick to his stomach. Erin grimaced when the gun sailed across the room and slammed against the wall. McKenzie tumbled backward over the coffee table.

Skip struggled to free himself from the handcuffs, but despite how loose they were, he couldn't quite pull his hands out, so he kicked the gun under the sofa.

McKenzie leaped up and yanked out an eight-inch baton. With the snap of his wrist, he extended it to its full length before swinging at Skip. Skip ducked and dodged the baton. McKenzie swung the stick at him repeatedly, backing him into a corner.

Erin cringed at the crack of the baton, and her son crumpled to the floor unconsciousness. Tears filled her eyes and flowed down her cheeks.

"Mr. McKenzie, please don't do this."

But McKenzie ignored her. Retrieving the gun from under the sofa, he aimed it at Skip.

Facing the Truth

Awakened from a sound sleep, Cassandra bolted upright in bed. Bounding from the bed, she flung open the door and flew down the steps to see what was happening. Her heart skipped a beat when she raced into the living room and saw Skip lying on the floor. Her dad stood over him with a gun, prepared to pull the trigger.

"No, Daddy, don't!"

For some strange reason, the thought of torturing the lad's mother by forcing her to watch him kill her son appealed to him, so he slowly aimed the gun at the boy, ignoring her pleas for him to spare her son's life. Ready to pull the trigger, Jason jumped when his daughter came flying out of nowhere and threw herself over top of the lad to protect him.

Jason promptly redirected his aim to avoid accidentally shooting her. "Cassandra, what are you doing here?"

Cassandra checked the boy's breathing and felt for a pulse. "Daddy, call an ambulance!" Leaping to her feet, she dashed toward the kitchen.

"No!" Jason cut her off. "I cut the phone lines, and you're not calling anybody."

"He's hurt!" Dropping beside young Shaughnessy, Cassandra burst into tears. "Oh, Skip. Daddy, why did you hurt him? You've always been kind and loving. Why did you do this?" She embraced the unconscious lad, tears spilling onto him when she buried her face in his shirt.

Jason raised an eyebrow. "Skip?" He watched how tenderly his daughter embraced the boy he'd considered to be his enemy. "Skip Shaughnessy."

With a sharp gasp, he deposited the gun in his holster and pulled out the New Testament that Cassandra had given him. He opened it and re-read the message. "Signed SS." Slowly closing the testament, Jason gazed uncertainly at Skip, pondering his initials. *Skip Shaughnessy.*

Re-pocketing the small Bible, Jason squatted beside his daughter. "Oh, no, Cassandra. Don't tell me that this is the boy you married."

Cassandra slowly nodded.

"Young lady, do you have any idea who he is? Do you?"

"Yes, Dad. He's the son of Stephen Shaughnessy and the one whose testimony convicted you." Cassandra's voice was soft and steady.

Jason narrowed his eyes and he could feel the heat rush to his face. "Then why did you marry him?"

"I love him." Tears spilled down her cheeks. "And he loves me."

Trembling with anger, his voice started to rise. "Does he know that you are *my* daughter?"

"Of course."

"Then how could you two possibly develop a close relationship?" yelled Jason. "Did it make no difference to you that you were dating the boy who sent me to prison?"

Despite his hostility toward her, Cassandra's reply remained calm. "Dad, I'm truly sorry that you went to prison, but can you honestly tell me that it's an unjust sentence? Did Skip tell the truth on the witness stand?"

That question pierced him through the heart. Skip not only told the truth, but Jason vividly recalled how frightened that boy looked when he took the stand. His conviction wasn't Skip's doing. There were a lot of little pieces that factored in. Young Shaughnessy just happened to be the final piece, the convicting factor, and Jason never forgave him for it. And for the first time since his conviction, he saw what he had become.

"Did he really witness that horrible crime?" said Cassandra. "He was still a boy when his dad was shot and killed."

Jason looked away. He couldn't bear to look his daughter in the face at this point.

"Well, did he tell the truth or not?"

"Um, yeah. He-he saw everything."

"What should he have done? If I had seen someone kill you, what would you want me to do?"

Jason knew that Cassandra was waiting for an answer, but he felt too ashamed to respond.

"Dad, I love you. I'm sorry that you're in prison. Skip and I pray for you every night. When Skip and I started dating, neither of us knew. By the time we realized it, we were too attached to each other to walk away from the relationship."

At the sound of soft footsteps, Jason turned. Through the living room doorway, he spied a young girl standing in the middle of the stairway. "Cassandra, who is that?"

"Skip's sister."

Jason caught a glimpse of Erin's terror-filled eyes.

Cassandra looked up at her young sister-in-law. "Stephanie, for your own safety, go back upstairs this instant, and don't come down until your mother or brother calls you."

Without a word, the girl sprinted back up the stairs.

Jason raised an eyebrow. "Cassandra, how could you even think that I would harm her?"

Cradling Skip, tears spilled down Cassandra's cheeks. "Dad, I didn't think for even a minute that you would deliberately harm anyone. I told Skip that he was being silly, that you weren't that kind of person. But I was wrong. You were going to kill him!"

Cassandra buried her face in Skip's shirt.

"You really love him, don't you?"

Cassandra nodded. "And he loves me. He'd do anything for me. The other night, I insisted that he run to the store to buy me some more hair spray. He was afraid because it was almost dark, and you hadn't been captured. I made a mockery of his fear."

"But he went anyway."

"Yes. I was so insistent on having that silly hair spray that I was going to go get it myself. But Skip didn't want me going out alone at night. So to make me happy, he ran to the store. He got mugged in the parking lot, and he got beat up. Oh, Dad, I felt so awful."

"Did he tell you who did it?"

Cassandra shook her head. "No. I overheard him tell his partner on the telephone that he had a clear shot, but he couldn't bring himself to pull the trigger."

Jason gazed down at the lad in his daughter's arms. He suddenly looked so young and innocent and vulnerable. And whether or not he liked it, this boy was now part of his family. "Cassie, what attracted you to him?"

"He's different, Dad. Different from any boy I've ever met."

"How so?"

"He's gentle and patient, but very strong. No matter how cruelly others treat him, he's always kind and forgiving."

Jason knew that was true, recalling how Skip attempted to bargain Morgan's release. *Then when I cornered him behind the supermarket, he had a clear shot for me, but he didn't take it. And while I'm trying to kill him, he spares my life. And after all the attempts I've made on his life, this evening he addressed me with respect.*

"Cassandra, I'm sorry for...um..." Jason looked away. "Never mind. I'm just sorry, that's all. I...uh..." His eyes met Cassandra's as he fumbled for the right words.

Cassandra gently lay Skip on the floor and grasped her father's hand. "It's okay, Dad. Skip is different because he's a Christian. I'm not nearly as patient or forgiving as he is, but I'm working on it."

"Your mother and sister?"

"Since they've accepted Jesus as their Savior, they've changed a lot. You'd hardly know them. They absolutely adore Skip, and they both know his testimony convicted you. Dad, are you ready to accept Jesus as your Savior?"

Pursing his lips, Jason shook his head. "God wouldn't want anything to do with a loser like me."

"God is no respecter of persons. The Bible says that God gives everyone who receives Him the power to become a child of God. Everyone, Dad. That means you."

"Cassandra, I couldn't live the Christian life. I could never be like Skip."

"No one expects you to be like Skip. Philippians 4:13 says, 'I can do all things through Christ which strengtheneth me.' That includes living the Christian life."

"Let me think about it." Withdrawing keys from his pocket, he unlocked the handcuffs that bound Skip's wrists and removed them.

"I love you, Dad, and I know you love me, but you don't have to put on an act of kindness for my sake. I just want the assurance that you won't bring any more harm to Skip or his family."

"This is no act, Cassandra. You made me face myself, and I didn't like what I saw. I'm truly sorry. Now, go untie Skip's mother."

Cassandra glanced over at her mother-in-law, back at her dad, and down at her husband. Skip lay on his side. Afraid to leave him with her dad so near, she rested her right hand on his head and slid the other one down to his tummy.

"It's okay, darling." Jason set his right hand on top of hers. "I won't hurt him again. I just want to get him off the hard floor." Lifting Skip into his arms, Jason carried him to the sofa.

Anxiously watching her dad, Cassandra scooted over to Erin, fumbling with the tightly knotted rope. A moment later, her dad dropped on his knees beside her.

"I'll untie his mother, darling. You take care of Skip."

Cassandra bounded out the door and dashed into the kitchen, returning a minute later with an icepack and a cold washcloth. Her father had re-holstered the gun and was wandering around the living room, studying the many family pictures on display while Erin knelt on the floor beside the sofa, running her fingers through Skip's hair. Cassandra handed her the icepack, and she pressed it against the knot on his head.

Squatting next to her, Cassandra spoke in a whisper. "Why don't you check on the girls? They must be frightened to death. I'll stay with Skip."

Erin rose to her feet and backed toward the stairs. When Jason made no attempt to stop her, she spun around and dashed up the stairs to her bedroom.

Cassandra washed Skip's face. Then she folded the wet washcloth and laid it on his forehead. "Skip, wake up." Cassandra gently shook him, but he didn't stir. "Skip?" Tears coursed down her cheeks as she sat beside him holding the icepack to his head.

Seating himself on the coffee table beside her, Jason took her hand. "Cassandra, don't worry about him. He'll be all right."

"But he's still unconscious."

"I really hit him hard, baby. Give him time to wake up. Okay?"

But Skip didn't move, and that worried her.

Erin returned twenty minutes later. Hurrying down the stairs, she trotted into the living room and glanced uneasily at Jason McKenzie, who was relaxing in her recliner.

"This is comfortable," he said. "We don't have anything like this in prison."

Joining Cassandra, Erin knelt beside Skip and ran her fingers through his hair. "I got the girls in bed."

Skip turned his head. "Dad?"

The ladies exchanged glances and looked at him.

"Dad?" said Cassandra. "Sweetheart, your dad is with Jesus."

Skip smiled in his sleep. "Yeah, but I'm going to see him."

"No!" Cassandra exploded into tears and pulled Skip into a crushing embrace. "Don't leave me."

Skip jumped at Cassandra's sudden outburst. Now, fully conscious, he slowly slid his arms around her, but Cassandra held him too tightly and cried too hard to notice.

"Shh, Cassandra." Skip rubbed her back. "Don't cry. I'm here."

Kissing him repeatedly, Cassandra squeezed him even tighter. "Promise me you'll never leave." Slowly releasing him, she sat up, gazing into his eyes and stroking his hair.

"That I'll never leave you?"

"You said that you're going to see your dad. You can't do that unless you die, and you were unconscious for so long that I was really worried about you."

"I must have been dreaming."

"How do you feel?"

"I have an awful headache." Skip started to sit up. A feeling of dread washed over him when he caught sight of McKenzie watching him. He glanced from his mother to Cassandra and back to McKenzie.

Erin settled onto the sofa beside him and pulled him into her arms as if to protect him.

"I'll bring you some aspirin, Angel." Cassandra patted his leg and hurried from the room.

Skip swallowed hard. His fearful gaze shifted from Cassandra to her dad, sitting there in a police uniform with a 40 caliber Glock in his holster. Likely, he had possession of Morgan's uniform and gun belt. Skip felt at his mercy, with no way to protect his family or defend himself against this man. He suspected that the only thing stopping him from withdrawing that gun and shooting them all was Cassandra's presence, but Cassandra had just left the room, and he wasn't about to take his eyes off McKenzie.

A moment later, Cassandra returned with two tablets and a cup of water. "Here, Angel. Take these."

Studying McKenzie uneasily, Skip downed the aspirin with a sip of water.

Jason found himself mesmerized by the good-looking boy that his daughter had married. *She calls him Angel.* As Jason thought back to how Skip spared his life while he was trying to kill the lad and how the boy attempted to bargain the release of a man who betrayed him, he thought how aptly the name fit him. *He's a good boy, and he's my son-in-law.* But Skip's steady gaze unnerved him.

"Hey, kid, don't look at me like that. I promised Cassandra that I wouldn't harm you. Okay?"

Skip continued to study him.

"Um, or...or your family, either. I'm sorry for threatening your mother." Jason paused, hoping for a response, but the lad remained silent, and his mother was still too frightened to talk.

Jason shifted his gaze, unable to keep eye contact with Skip's piercing blue eyes. "Look, son, you married my daughter, Cassandra. Whether or not you like it, that makes you the son-in-law of a convict, particularly at this moment, an escaped convict. Now, when you married my precious daughter, you made an excellent choice for a wife. Unfortunately, you're stuck with a no-good convict for a father-in-law."

"That's true, but I'll bet you'll raise more eyebrows telling your buddies that your son-in-law is a cop than I do telling my friends that my father-in-law is a convict."

"Do your friends know?"

"Indeed, they do. May I ask you something, Mr. McKenzie? How did you get to my house without the police stopping you?"

Drumming his fingers nervously, Jason forced a smile. "That was easy. It's dark out. I drove up in a Forest Valley police cruiser, and I got out wearing a police uniform. They're looking for a convict, not a cop."

"Oh. Well, you're now under arrest, so surrender your weapon peacefully."

Chapter 32

Skip Takes Charge

Jason raised an eyebrow. He couldn't believe what he just heard. With absolutely no means to back his authority as a police officer, Cassandra's angel just arrested him.

Sitting on either side of Skip, the two ladies both caught their breath. The lad had no gun or any way to subdue or apprehend an armed convict if he refused to comply. And Jason could tell by their responses that they both expected him to resist.

He scrutinized Skip for a moment, wondering what the lad would do if he disobeyed. "And if I don't?"

"Don't make me come over there."

Jason glanced from his daughter to his son-in-law. In the short time he'd known the lad, he'd learned a lot about his character, and everything that Cassandra had said about him was unbelievably true, so Jason had no reason to think that Skip made idle threats.

If he refused to obey a lawful order from a police officer, he'd be forcing a confrontation, because he had no doubt, at this point, that Skip would confront him. Then Jason would have to submit to the lad or fight, and if he fought, someone would get hurt, possibly his precious daughter. Because she would fight to protect Skip. So where did that leave him? Either way, he was going back to prison. Why make it harder on himself or Cassandra.

Slowly withdrawing the gun from Morgan's holster, he quietly laid it on the floor and slid it over to Skip. Skip leaned down and scooped it up.

"Any other weapons?"

Jason shook his head. "No, son, not even a pocket knife."

Holding the gun loosely, Skip stood. "Now where are you holding Morgan?"

Jason studied him curiously. "Are you sure you want to know? He's a real scumbag. He obtained your address for me, or I wouldn't be here right now. Although, in all fairness to him, I did have a gun pointed at his head. That made him a might nervous and very compliant."

"You don't like him, do you?" asked Skip.

"Do you?"

"No, sir, I don't. But for me to treat him like he's treated me would make me no different than he is, and I shall not lower myself to his valueless standards."

Jason smiled. "Point well taken. I have him tied up in the motel near the supermarket."

"Which one?" asked Skip. "There are about four motels near that supermarket."

"Um..." Jason's mind went blank. "It's the one that... No, no, not that one." He thought for a moment. "Well, there's a room in the back..." He drew a circle in the air. "If you go down the corridor and around the corner, there it is."

Skip looked at Cassandra. "Does your dad always give directions like that?"

Cassandra burst into laughter. "Only when he's nervous."

"I know right where it is," said Jason. "If you'll take me with you..."

"No!" exclaimed Erin and Cassandra in unison.

Skip glanced from his wife to his mother.

"I don't trust him, Skip," said Erin.

"Neither do I," said Cassandra.

Jason raised an eyebrow, hurt by his daughter's statement.

"I'm sorry, Dad. You lost my confidence when you exploded through that door and threatened to kill my husband."

"Skip, run out to the patrol car and radio for a unit to come get this man," said his mother. "Then inform the police of the plight of the other officer, and send *them* to search for him. You are off duty. Let the duty officers handle this situation."

Skip looked at his mother in surprise. "Mom, you're not serious! An opportunity like this comes around once in a police career, and you want to deprive me of handling it myself? Oh, my gosh! To recapture an escaped convict and rescue a fellow officer at the same time is an opportunity I'm *not* passing along to another officer. Especially the rescue part. We're talking about Morgan, and I want to see the look on his face when *I* come through that door to free him."

"Let me go with you," said Jason. "I want to be there, too. He betrayed me a long time before he betrayed you."

"Where are the handcuffs?" asked Skip.

Jason withdrew them from the case on Morgan's gun belt.

"Put them on, and you may go."

Erin looked from her son to Jason. "No, Skip, please don't take him with you. He's dangerous and unpredictable."

Jason locked the handcuffs onto his wrists.

Cassandra bounded to her feet. "I'm going with you."

"I'd rather you didn't," said Skip.

"Do you want me to stay home crying and worrying?"

Jason glanced from the pleading look on his daughter's face, to his son-in-law's expression. The thought of leaving her home crying obviously bothered him. *He loves her tremendously.* That realization warmed Jason's heart.

Skip glanced from his concerned mother to his worried wife. "Mom, will you feel better if Cassandra's with me?"

"Yes."

"All right." Grasping Jason's arm, Skip escorted him out to the patrol car parked at the curb. Cassandra walked on the other side of her father.

"The keys are in my left pants pocket," said Jason.

Skip retrieved the car keys and seated him in the cage of the police car. Then he opened the front passenger's door for Cassandra. Cassandra slid into the car and Skip kissed her before closing the door. Jason grinned as he watched Skip hustle around to the driver's side and jump behind the wheel. He cranked the engine and pulled away from the curb.

Jason directed Skip to his motel hideout. Skip parked the car next to Fred Brewster's Oldsmobile.

"Mr. Brewster is going to be really happy to see his car," said Skip.

Hustling around the police car, Skip opened the front passenger's door for Cassandra and the back door for Jason, escorting them into the motel room. The instant they entered the room, a foul stench greeted them.

"Oo." Skip crinkled his nose as he hit the light switch.

Cassandra trailed him into her dad's motel room. "Pee-ewe, it stinks in here!" She waved her hand in front of her face, attempting to clear the air.

Drooping against his restraints, Morgan's bloodshot eyes wearily looked up when they entered the room. His briefs were drenched and he sat on a yellow puddle-saturated carpet. Jason grinned at him and plopped down on the unmade bed.

Despite his circumstances, Morgan blushed at the sight of Jason's daughter. Cassandra's big brown eyes widened at the sight of him. Skip squatted beside him and unlocked the handcuffs, removing them from Brent's chafed wrists.

"You all right?"

With his hands finally free, Brent ripped the tape from his mouth. "Ahh!" He cried out in pain when the tape yanked his facial hair.

Jason laughed at the grimace on Skip's face, expressing the mere thought of the pain behind Morgan's yell. But the lad's face was so smooth, it looked like he didn't shave yet.

"Oh, that must have hurt," said Skip.

"You wouldn't know!"

"That's true."

Morgan loosened the rope that bound his ankles and kicked it off. He glanced over at Jason and back at Skip. "Thanks. How did you know where to find me?"

"Mr. McKenzie told me."

"Who's the girl?"

Standing, Skip pulled Cassandra into his arms and snuggled up to her. "This is my beautiful wife, Cassandra." Skip kissed Cassandra's cheek, and she beamed. "Cassie, I'd like you to meet Officer Brent Morgan."

"Morgan? You're the officer who constantly harasses Skip?"

Glancing down at his meager attire, Brent blushed. "You had to bring your wife with you."

"I didn't want her to worry about me. After all that's happened lately, if I had left her home, she'd be crying her eyes out, afraid something would happen to me. So I brought her along."

Jason had wanted to be there when young Shaughnessy showed up to free the very officer who sold him out, but the best part of this rescue was watching his daughter and son-in-law together. Cassandra absolutely adored him, and he treated her so well.

Slowly getting to his feet, Morgan leaned against the wall to steady himself. Glaring at Jason, he said, "Give me back my uniform."

With a grin, Jason held up his handcuffed wrists.

"Shaughnessy, uncuff him so he can take off my uniform."

"Afraid not. He's an escaped convict in my custody. I'm not removing those handcuffs until I get him to jail." Skip grabbed Jason's discarded blue jeans off the floor and tossed them to Morgan. "Here, put these on. You'll get your uniform back later."

As he stepped into the jeans, Morgan glared at Jason.

With a wink, Jason leaned toward him and spoke softly. "You'll never wear this uniform again."

Chapter 33

Code Three

Brent paused, glancing at Skip to see if he'd overheard McKenzie's comment, but he gave no indication. Cassandra watched him with amusement when he slipped into the jeans and pulled them over top of his saturated underwear. With a grimace, he snapped and zipped them.

Boy is this uncomfortable. Brent turned to Skip. "Did you radio for back up?"

"No need. Are you all right, or do you want an ambulance?"

"No. I just need a good meal and a hot shower. Will you run me home on the way to the station?"

Grasping McKenzie's arm, Skip led him out the door to the police car, seating him in the back seat. Brent pushed Cassandra aside and reached for the front passenger's door, but quick as lightening, Skip intercepted it, motioning for Cassandra to climb in.

"Shouldn't you come down to the station and file a report?" asked Skip.

Seeing Cassandra slide into the front seat, Brent sighed and reluctantly crawled into the back with McKenzie. "I will, but I want to shower and eat first."

Cassandra crinkled her nose and waved her hand to clear the air. "You definitely need a shower."

He knew he did. He could smell himself, and the odor was horrendous.

Sliding behind the wheel of the police car, Skip started the ignition and immediately lowered all four windows before pulling out into traffic.

"Are you certain you want McKenzie to see where you live? Thanks to you, he has my address. You want to give him yours, too?"

No! What was he thinking? And to make matters worse, he had to be reminded of the stupidity of it by the department's kiddy cop.

"On second thought, I think I'll shower and change at the station."

"You're a brave officer," said Skip.

"What do you mean by that?"

Skip didn't reply.

Brent glared at him through the cage.

"How does it feel to ride back here like a criminal?" asked Jason.

"Well, at least I'm not handcuffed. How did our kiddy cop overpower you anyway?"

Jason narrowed his eyes and spoke softly. "He didn't overpower me. I surrendered to him, but despite his youth, he's a better cop than you'll ever be. I had run-ins with both of you, and look who came out on top. If it weren't for the lad you betrayed, you'd be dead right now, because after I killed him, I intended to shoot you."

Brent glanced at Skip to see if he caught any of their discussion, but he didn't seem to be listening. He was talking to Cassandra.

"Skip, this is so fun. I've never ridden in a police car before."

"If you had to drive one every day, you'd get tired of it." Skip coasted into a service station and stopped at the gas pump. "Do you have some money or a credit card?" he asked Cassandra. "I need to put a few dollars into the gas tank to get us back to the station. I'll never make it across town on empty."

Cassandra handed him six dollars. "Sorry, that's all I have left out of that twenty you gave me."

"Thanks," said Skip. "This will be plenty." Skip stepped from the car.

Brent's gaze followed him. Crossing his arms tightly, he shoved his trembling hands into his armpits as he watched Skip through the window. "You intended to shoot me anyway? Why? I gave you what you wanted."

"Did you? You think that betraying innocent blood is really what I wanted?"

Brent sighed. "I guess not. The day you killed Stephen Shaughnessy, he cornered me in the parking lot of the police station as he was leaving work. He told me that he had reason to believe I was dealing drugs and that he was launching an investigation first thing in the morning."

Brent glanced from Cassandra, who turned in her seat to hear what he was saying, to Skip, who hurried inside the convenience store to pay for the gas.

Jason raised an eyebrow. "You mean, if I hadn't been a fool and robbed that store, turning the shotgun on him, you might be in prison instead of me?"

Watching Skip through the large glass window, Brent nodded. "Shaughnessy didn't get to be our assistant police chief accidentally. And there was no doubt that he would make police chief. He was sharp. I knew he had me, and I hated him for it. He died before that investigation was launched. Boy was I relieved."

"I'll bet you were. You got off scot free, and I went to prison for murder."

"The following week, my partner got caught stealing confiscated contraband and went to jail. That's when I got out of the dope business. I didn't want to go to jail."

"Well, I didn't mean to kill anybody. I panicked when I saw that uniform, and I pulled the trigger. But, at this point, I'm ashamed that I sought revenge on his innocent son for doing nothing more than getting on the witness stand and telling what he saw."

Cringing at Jason's description of Skip, Brent knew that he was guilty of the same thing. Through the store window, he could see Skip leaning on the counter, talking to the clerk.

"I was glad that Shaughnessy died that day," said Brent. "I was so afraid that Stephen would learn the truth and I would go to prison, that when Skip joined the police department two years later, I took my hostility out on him anyway I could get away with it. That kid is every bit as sharp as his dad, and I've been scared to death that Skip would learn the truth."

Jason gazed at Brent. "You've been in a prison, too. I never realized that before. Your prison was one of fear and guilt." Shifting his gaze, Jason glanced from the girl to her approaching husband. "That boy's something else. Brent, after what you did to him, he asked me to release you."

Brent's eyes widened, and he looked from Skip to Jason. "No way. You didn't tell him everything, did you?"

"You bet I did. You're a traitor. Not only did you betray me, but you betrayed Skip, a fellow officer, and I wanted him to know it."

The driver's door opened. Skip slid behind the wheel, started the ignition, and pulled out of the service station.

"Skip, what took you so long?" asked Cassandra.

"Oh, I was just talking to Benjie. He'd heard about escaped convicts in the area and wanted to know if the two guys in the cage were escapees I was returning to prison."

"What did you tell him?" asked Brent.

"Now what do you think I told him? I said that one guy is an escaped convict and the other one is a crooked cop."

Jason laughed. "Boy, has he got you pegged!"

"Skip, did you really tell him that?" asked Cassandra.

"No, Cassie. Actually, Benjie was telling me about his weekend fishing trip. I didn't want to be rude. That's why I was inside so long. Sorry."

"Take your time," said Jason. "I'm not in any hurry to go back to prison."

"Well, I want to shower and change," said Brent. "And I haven't eaten in two days, so step on it. In fact, hit your lights and sirens, and let's get there really fast."

"You're not serious," said Skip. "Your need to shower and eat is not an emergency, and I am *not* going code three."

He was right, and Brent knew it. But it burned him for a patrol officer to usurp his authority as sergeant. Especially *this* patrol officer. And he wasn't about to let that happen. "Code three, Shaughnessy. Now! That's an order."

Skip shook his head. "Okay, but don't say I didn't warn you." He flipped on his lights and siren before accelerating up to 65 miles per hour.

Cassandra grinned as they raced across town. Leaning toward Skip, she touched his arm. "Will you be in trouble for this?"

"I won't. I'm a patrol officer following orders. Morgan is the sergeant who issued them, and he'll have a lot of explaining to do."

Reaching the police station in record time, Skip braked to a screeching halt at the main entrance, but before he had time to throw the cruiser into park, Captain Kramer and several officers raced from the building.

"Shaun, what on earth..." The captain's voice trailed off when he spotted Morgan in the cage of the cruiser with McKenzie.

"Sorry, Captain." Skip spoke through Cassandra's open window. "I was ordered to get here code three."

"By whom?"

Skip nodded toward his caged colleague as another officer opened the cruiser's back door for him.

"Oh, my gosh! What is that stench?" cried Charlie.

"Morgan!" The other officers immediately stepped back, giving him a wide berth.

"Did you wet your pants?" asked Greg. "You smell like a pee factory,"

"Morgan, where have you been for the last two days?" said Captain Kramer. "How come an escaped convict is wearing your uniform? And since when do you pull rank on Shaughnessy by ordering him to go code three on a routine run?"

Brent stepped from the cruiser. "Um...well, I...I mean, he..."

"You were a sergeant before I joined this department, so I don't know how you got those stripes, but first thing tomorrow morning, you're going before the review board to see if you keep them. Now go shower and change. You stink!"

Watching the scenario from his cruiser, Skip stifled his laughter when the captain turned his back on Brent and trotted into the station.

Greg chuckled. "Boy, Morgan, you need a diaper change."

"Shut up!"

"And it's obvious where you've been," said Charlie. "McKenzie is wearing your uniform. What happened? Did our kiddy cop have to rescue you?"

The other guys started laughing.

"Hey, Morgan, it's certain you'll lose those sergeant's stripes. The captain insists all sergeants be potty trained," said Tim.

Greg shook his head in disbelief. "I guess you guys haven't heard. A new ruling was just passed that requires *all* officers be potty trained, not just sergeants. They are really cracking down."

"You're kidding!" gasped Charlie. "Boy, do they expect a lot from us."

"Very funny!" Brent shoved them aside, stomping up the stairs and into the station.

Skip laughed as he made a u-turn in the parking lot and drove around to the closed garage. Pulling up to a security keypad, he reached through his open window and punched in the code. The garage door opened. Skip coasted inside and closed the garage door behind them.

Entering the police station through a side door, Skip locked up Morgan's gun and escorted his prisoner down a short hallway, which led directly to the jail. Cassandra followed them. Skip opened the cell door before freeing McKenzie from handcuffs.

McKenzie watched his daughter as he quietly stepped into the cell. Without warning, he grabbed Skip's arm and yanked him into the jail cell. When the metal door clanged shut, it locked Skip inside.

Chapter 34

The Truth Comes Out

Startled, Skip dropped the keys on the floor. But before he had a chance to pick them up, McKenzie grabbed his arm and pulled him to the far end of the jail cell. Skip glanced back at Cassandra.

"Dad!" Cassandra shook the bars. "Don't you hurt him!" She reached through the bars to retrieve the keys, but they lay just beyond reach.

"Skip, I want to thank you for sparing my life the other night and for not telling my daughter who beat you up."

"Dad!" Cassandra rattled the bars again. "What are you telling him?"

Skip smiled. "You're welcome, sir."

"Son, I never thought I'd say this, but I greatly respect you. Cassandra picked a winner, and I know you'll take good care of her. Now what can we do about Morgan?"

Skip cocked his head. "Sir?"

"I don't suppose you can still arrest him for pushing drugs a few years back? I'd be glad to testify."

"I'm afraid the evidence is long gone. With no evidence, it would be your word against his, and unfortunately, you would not be considered a credible witness."

"Well, that man's a traitor! He betrayed me four years ago, and I went to prison. But this time, he betrayed a fellow officer and nearly got him killed. Surely there's something we can do."

Skip smiled. "There is. I'll be right back."

Leaving Jason, Skip scooped up the keys, reached through the bars, and unlocked the jail cell door from the outside.

"Skip, what were you and my father talking about?" asked Cassandra.

Skip kissed her. "You. He said to take good care of his little girl."

Cassandra beamed and smiled at her dad

Taking her hand, Skip led his young wife out of the jail and cornered Greg, who was getting ready to go on patrol. "Would you run Cassandra home for me? I have some things I got to take care of, so I'll be here for awhile."

"No problem."

Skip cupped her chin and kissed her cheek. "I know you're tired."

Cassandra yawned. "That's an understatement."

"And you can assure Mom that I'm all right and let her know where I am, because I'll probably be here for awhile."

"You bet." With a weary smile, Cassandra grasped Skip's hand. "I owe you an apology. I never thought that my dad would deliberately harm anyone, not even you. But the night you got mugged in the supermarket parking lot, you were fighting with my dad, weren't you?"

"Um..." Skip shuffled his feet and looked away. "What makes you ask that?"

For a long, silent moment, Cassandra studied his face. "Why didn't you tell me?"

Skip gazed into her warm brown eyes. "You believed my fears were unfounded. How could I force you to understand what I was going through?"

Massaging Skip's hand, Cassandra's eyes glistened with tears. "Skip, I am so sorry that you had to go through that ordeal without my support and strength."

Skip smiled at her. "Don't worry about it. God provided me with His support and strength. I'll see you at home."

Cassandra left with Greg, and Skip hurried to locate his captain before he left the station for the night. Despite the lateness of the hour, Skip found him in his office. The light was on and his door was open, so Skip tapped on the door and quietly entered.

Captain Kramer looked up when he walked in.

"Boy, you're working real late tonight," said Skip.

"Yeah, and from the looks of things, I might be here for another hour before I can go home. What do you need?"

Skip cringed. "Sorry, Captain. I hate to pile more work on you, but I was at the motel where McKenzie was hiding out. Fred Brewster's Oldsmobile is parked out back. In his car, he had firearms and ammunition. I'd imagine they're in the motel room. We need to rope off that section of the motel with crime scene tape, and detectives need to get out there as soon as possible."

Kramer nodded. "That's for sure. Which motel is it?" Kramer handed him a pen and notepad. "Jot down the name of the motel and its location."

Once he finished writing, Skip looked up at his captain expectantly.

"Anything else?"

"Um...about Morgan..."

"Morgan's busted, and nothing you say will change my mind."

"Yes, sir, and you need to know that he obtained my address for McKenzie, which nearly got me killed."

Captain Kramer bounded to his feet. "He did what?"

"Mr. McKenzie will tell you the whole story."

"Go get Morgan and meet me at the jail. I'll be there as soon as I get the ball rolling on that stolen merchandise at the motel."

It wasn't a long flight, but it had been an incredibly long day. While the boys gathered their luggage from the carousel, Rose tried to call Erin again, but the phone just rang.

"This has me concerned," said Rose. "We'd better get straight to their house. I hope everything's all right."

It was nearly a thirty minute drive from the airport, but when Rose finally turned into their driveway, she saw lights on in the house.

Without knocking, they entered the house.

"Erin?" called Rose.

"In the kitchen."

While the boys brought in their luggage, Rose darted into the kitchen. The ladies hugged.

"Oh, I've been so worried about you," said Rose. "I've been trying to call you all day."

"Yeah, our phone lines were cut. I don't know what delayed your return, but thank God it was delayed. Boy, have I got a lot to tell you."

Skip located Brent in the locker room. Freshly showered and dressed in clean clothes, Morgan reluctantly followed him back to the jail.

"You said Kramer wanted to see me. Where is he?"

"He'll be here in a minute," said Skip. "He had something important he needed to take care of first."

"Yeah, well I'm not waitin'. I think you're just making this up."

"It's your funeral," said Skip. "I'm just the messenger."

With a sigh, Brent glanced over at McKenzie and back at Skip, but he didn't leave.

A few minutes later, Kramer joined them. He gave Brent a long, hard gaze, making him squirm uncomfortably.

Finally, Brent said, "You wanted to see me, Captain?"

"Yes. What's this I hear about you obtaining Skip's address for an escaped convict out to kill him?"

"What?" cried Brent. "Who told you that?"

"Skip did."

Kramer's expression turned hard as he silently studied Brent.

Skip glanced from Kramer to Morgan to McKenzie. No one spoke.

Brent swallowed hard. "Look, I would never do such a thing. McKenzie asked me for it, but..."

"He asked you for it?" echoed Kramer. "You're a cop! Why didn't you arrest him and bring him in?"

Brent didn't answer, so Jason spoke up. "I had him at gunpoint. I made him give me his uniform before I handcuffed him." He spoke through the bars as he elaborated on how Morgan had so readily offered information about Skip to save himself.

"No! He...He's lying! I don't know how he found out where Shaughnessy lives, but it wasn't from me."

Kramer put his hands on his hips. "So he threatened to kill you, but you didn't tell him anything. He coincidentally set up shop clear across town within walking distance of Skip's home without any guidance from you."

"That's...that's right."

"And then he conned you into going to the supermarket clear across town and abducted you at gunpoint. He held you prisoner for two days, at which time you never told him a thing, and he accidentally found Skip's house and broke down the back door."

"Well, I don't know how he found Skip's house, but I didn't tell him."

"Of course, you didn't. He stopped and asked directions from a police officer."

Skip started laughing.

"Shut up, Shaughnessy! This isn't funny!" yelled Brent.

Captain Kramer stifled a laugh himself. "No. What's really funny is that Skip ended up going in to save *you*. If it weren't for these two, you'd still be sitting there tied up. You might as well admit it, Brent, because you're only fooling yourself. However, if it will make you feel any better, I'll arrange for you both to take a polygraph test."

"What!" cried Brent. "Why should I?"

"I'll take it," said Jason. "This scoundrel betrayed my son-in-law. He's not worthy to wear that uniform."

"I see no reason to take a polygraph test due to these ludicrous allegations! I refuse."

"You're through, Morgan. Clean out your locker and turn in your equipment."

"Captain, you're not serious! This is a frame up. Shaughnessy's lying, like he always does. And it's my word against his."

"Now you're blaming Skip? Fine. You hold onto your job. As of this moment, you're on administrative leave, without pay, pending an investigation. But don't fret. Internal Affairs will launch their investigation first thing in the morning. And they'll get to the bottom of everything, including the criminal charges that can be brought against you."

Morgan's eyebrows shot up to his hairline. "Criminal charges?" Clearing his throat, he forced a smile. "Never mind. It's not important. I'll just clean out my locker and turn in my equipment."

"Right now!" commanded Paul.

"Yes, sir. Right now." Spinning on his heel, Brent disappeared down the hall.

Jason turned to Skip. "Son, I owe you an apology. When I was convicted, I was angry at the world. And my hit-list consisted of anyone whom I felt had anything to do with separating me from my family. Because your testimony played a major role in my conviction, your name was at the top of that list. Cassandra made me see how wrong I was to blame you. Morgan got me started on drugs, and I hate him for it."

Paul raised an eyebrow. "No wonder he didn't want Internal Affairs investigating him."

"He's corrupt and disloyal. It burned me to see him still masquerading as a police officer while I served time. Thanks, Skip, I appreciate what you just did. You got him dismissed from the police department. I never could have accomplished that alone."

"You did it, Mr. McKenzie."

"I may have told your captain what happened, but he only listened because I had your word backing me."

"That's exactly right," said Paul.

"And, Skip, I would appreciate it if you stopped calling me Mr. McKenzie. Like it or not, we're now family. Why don't you call me Jason?"

Reaching through the bars, Jason grasped Skip's hand in friendship.

"Um..." Skip choked on his words. "Yes, sir. I got to go. I still have a report to write."

As Skip turned to leave, he glanced back at Cassandra's father. The last person in the world he had ever expected to befriend was Jason McKenzie, his father's murderer.

Your Eternity Awaits

Do You Know Jesus?

"For this is good and acceptable in the sight of God our Saviour;

Who will have all men to be saved, and to come unto the knowledge of the truth.

For there is one God, and one mediator between God and men, the man Christ Jesus."

I Timothy 2:3-5

Titus 2:11 says, **"For the grace of God that bringeth salvation hath appeared to all men."**

God is perfect, and He created mankind in His image.

Adam and Eve, the first man and woman, were created in perfection. They were perfect because God their Creator is perfect. And because of God's holiness, He cannot have fellowship with sinful people.

So when Adam and Eve sinned, all of God's creation immediately fell into a sinful state, and all babies were born with a sinful nature.

Romans 5:12 says, **"Wherefore, as by one man sin entered into the world, and death by sin; and so death passed upon all men, for that all have sinned."**

As a result, we were separated from our holy Creator.

Romans 3:23 says, **"For all have sinned, and come short of the glory of God."**

Then Romans 6:23 says, **"For the wages of sin is death ..."**

Sin has a penalty – Death.

Everyone dies physically. That's the *first* death.

Revelation 20:14-15 says, **"And death and hell were cast into the lake of fire. This is the second death. And whosoever was not found written in the book of life was cast into the lake of fire."**

But God sent His Son to pay your penalty!

Romans 6:23 says, **"For the wages of sin is death; but the gift of God is eternal life through Jesus Christ our Lord."**

I Corinthians 15:3-4 says, **"For I delivered unto you first of all that which I also received, how that Christ died for our sins according to the scriptures; and that he was buried, and that he rose again the third day according to the scriptures."**

And God wishes none should perish. Not even you! So he made a way for you to escape eternal damnation in hell.

"For God so loved the world, that he gave his only begotten Son, that whosoever believeth in him should not perish, but have everlasting life." John 3:16

All You Have to do is Confess and Believe

Romans 10:9-10 says ...

"That if thou shalt confess with thy mouth the Lord Jesus, and shalt believe in thine heart that God hath raised him from the dead, thou shalt be saved.

For with the heart man believeth unto righteousness; and with the mouth, confession is made unto salvation."

Only those who accept Jesus as their Savior will have their names written in the Lamb's Book of Life. It's not a book of the names of every soul who's ever lived. No. It's God's *Book of Eternal Life,* containing the names of every soul who's trusted His Son as Savior.

But How Do I Get Saved?

1. Admit that you're a sinner and that you can't save yourself.

2. Believe in the Lord Jesus Christ

3. Confess and repent of your sins.

"For whosoever shall call upon the name of the Lord shall be saved." Romans 10:13

"And as it is appointed unto men once to die, but after this the judgment." Hebrews 9:27

Preview of Book 6:

Preview of Book 6:

Skip Shaughnessy on The Brink of Disaster

He's a protector. In an effort to protect others, will he inadvertently sacrifice himself?

Skip Shaughnessy could lose his job and his freedom. Under the crushing weight of supporting his family financially and emotionally, Skip is falsely accused. But he's devastated when his mother adamantly rejects him as protector of his family.

Deciding he's no longer needed at home, he takes his wife hunting for their own apartment. But when Skip aids a young woman being stalked, he discovers her dad is the ex-convict his mom has befriended.

Can he protect the girl from the men after her or will he die in the attempt?

Other Books Written by Marjorie Strebe

Books in Skip's Action Series

Skip Shaughnessy in Keeping Secrets (Book 1)

Skip Shaughnessy in The Truth Shall Make You Free (Book 2)

Skip Shaughnessy in A Way to Escape (Book 3)

Skip Shaughnessy and The Surprise Family Union (Book 4)

Treasures in My Spiritual Hope Chest
Volumes 1 & 2

A King James devotional book with scripturally-sound lessons to help you grow spiritually when you read, understand, and apply God's Word to your life. You will discover priceless nuggets of God's truth in each devotional.

Another Day; Another Challenge

The Biography of a Child with Williams Syndrome
Third Edition

A special needs child with a mental handicap and developmental delays is falling through the cracks of every service designed to support her needs.

For more information, visit www.marjiestrebe.com, or me at kjvwriter@marjiestrebe.com.

9 798990 213654